An Image Of Isobel
Flicked Into His Mind.

And just like that he was taut as a bow. Aching and thinking all kinds of inappropriate thoughts.

Why couldn't he get his mind off a woman who was wrong for him in every way? Who challenged him on every level?

Frustrated, he went into the bathroom for a glass of water. Something that would slake the thirst that made him crave so much more than a long draw of liquid.

She'd be leaving soon, and that was a good thing, he told himself.

But the thought of never seeing her again made his body ache and turned his mind to the night they'd shared. He wanted more. He wanted that sensation of having his senses scattered to the wind. He wanted, even for the briefest time, to give himself over fully to the moment.

He wanted Isobel Fyfe.

Dear Reader,

Welcome to the third story in The Master Vintners series. While in Adelaide in May 2010, when I sat having lunch in an Italian restaurant with a friend and dreaming up the first two TMV books, I never imagined that it would lead me to fall in love with a whole new population of characters. The extended Masters family, and their offshoot of friends, have provided my imagination with challenges and story ideas that have kept me occupied for some time.

I was lucky enough to visit a few of the vineyards outside of Adelaide and to admire the beautiful settings, taste the carefully crafted and delicious wines and bask in the ambience of all that is amazing when you visit a country that is not your own. It seemed only fitting, to me, to give those stunning vistas and experiences a longer life in my own heart and mind than the short time I was able to be there.

In *One Secret Night,* Ethan Masters discovers a shocking family secret. It's a measure of how difficult he finds this information to deal with when he uncharacteristically divulges it to a woman he meets only in passing, and expects never to see again. Their secret night turns into a firestorm of passion and emotion as he and free-spirited Isobel Fyfe learn what it's like when opposites attract… and fall in love.

I hope you'll fall in love with Ethan and Isobel, too!

Happy reading,

Yvonne Lindsay

YVONNE
LINDSAY

ONE SECRET NIGHT

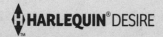

HARLEQUIN® DESIRE

Recycling programs
for this product may
not exist in your area.

ISBN-13: 978-0-373-73230-2

ONE SECRET NIGHT

Printed in U.S.A.

Books by Yvonne Lindsay

Harlequin Desire

   Bought: His Temporary Fiancée #2078
   The Pregnancy Contract #2117
††*The Wayward Son* #2141
††*A Forbidden Affair* #2147
   A Silken Seduction #2180
   A Father's Secret #2187
††*One Secret Night* #2217

Silhouette Desire

 The Boss's Christmas Seduction #1758
 The CEO's Contract Bride #1776
 The Tycoon's Hidden Heir #1788
  Rossellini's Revenge Affair #1811
  Tycoon's Valentine Vendetta #1854
  Jealousy & A Jewelled Proposition #1873
  Claiming His Runaway Bride #1890
†*Convenient Marriage, Inconvenient Husband* #1923
†*Secret Baby, Public Affair* #1930
†*Pretend Mistress, Bona Fide Boss* #1937
  Defiant Mistress, Ruthless Millionaire #1986
****Honor-Bound Groom* #2029
****Stand-In Bride's Seduction* #2038
****For the Sake of the Secret Child* #2044

 *New Zealand Knights
†Rogue Diamonds
**Wed at Any Price
††The Master Vintners

Other titles by this author available in ebook format.

YVONNE LINDSAY

New Zealand born, to Dutch immigrant parents, Yvonne Lindsay became an avid romance reader at the age of thirteen. Now, married to her "blind date" and with two fabulous children, she remains a firm believer in the power of romance. Yvonne feels privileged to be able to bring to her readers the stories of her heart. In her spare time, when not writing, she can be found with her nose firmly in a book, reliving the power of love in all walks of life. She can be contacted via her website, www.yvonnelindsay.com.

This book is dedicated to dear friends who helped me
brainstorm when my brain was a tranquil place
with nothing happening—a lovely thing to have
but not when you're nutting out a plot!
Nalini, Peta and Shar—big thanks for all your help.

One

His mother was alive.

Ethan Masters walked blindly through Adelaide's city streets, the staggering knowledge continuing to ricochet in his mind. A mind already struggling to come to terms with his father's recent unexpected death. He'd thought that would be the hardest thing he would ever have to face. But this discovery today, that the man Ethan had idolized and revered above all others had lied to him and his sister for the past twenty-five years, was much worse.

Grief mingled with a sharp sense of betrayal sliced through him anew—its blade serrated and leaving behind a raw pain that throbbed incessantly deep inside his chest. He didn't know what to do with the information he'd been given today. Part of him wished he'd never learned the truth. In fact, if he hadn't discovered an anomaly in his father's personal accounts he would still be none the wiser. The family solicitor's reluctance to explain had only made him more determined to discover where the monthly payments had been going.

So, now he knew. The woman who had abandoned him and his sister, Tamsyn, had accepted money to stay away, happy to let her children think she'd died in the car accident that had spared their lives.

Even worse, his father's siblings, Ethan's uncle Edward and aunt Cynthia, had colluded in the lie.

It went against everything—*every* family institution— he'd been brought up with. Bad enough that his memories of his parents had been tainted. But to know that so many people he trusted had gone behind his back…it was more than he could take. Maybe he should have gone straight home after his meeting in the city—confronted his aunt and uncle, told Tamsyn the truth. But if he himself found it next to impossible to weigh the information he'd received today, how could he expect to face his sister with the news?

The very idea of telling Tamsyn sent a shudder down his spine. Tamsyn was, by nature, a caretaker. She wanted everyone to be happy, and she worked darn hard to achieve that goal. Always had, even as a child. It was one of the reasons why her branch of the family business was so sought after and came so highly recommended. This news could well destroy her. He couldn't bear to see that happen. He hadn't spent the past twenty-five years of his life being her champion to fall at this hurdle now. No, this was his problem to deal with and he needed to work out his next move before facing everyone. He'd reach that decision a darn sight faster without the various demands of the family business, not to mention his extended family buzzing around to distract him.

A flicker of exotic color and movement caught his eye. A young woman who stood out from all the somber office workers marking the end of their working week by spilling from nearby buildings. Small, slender and blond, her dress a multihued swirl that clung briefly to outline her buttocks and thighs as a passing vehicle threw a gust of air in her direction. An incongruously large and cumbersome pack was settled on her back, yet she carried it as if it weighed nothing at all. Intrigued, Ethan watched as she slipped through the doors of a nearby pub and out of sight.

Without a second thought, Ethan followed her footsteps. He pulled himself up short as he entered the building and firmed his lips into a grim line. For someone who hadn't wanted distraction he'd certainly found it in the noisy confusion of pub patrons—a blend of tourists, students and office workers. For a second, he considered leaving. But what the hell, maybe concentration would come more smoothly after a drink. Straightening his shoulders, he headed to the bar. He scanned the crowd all the while, but he saw no sign of the colorful butterfly that had drawn him here.

Minutes later, Ethan listened to the beat of the music energizing the people on the dance floor—people whose lives were clearly far less complicated than his had so rapidly become—and deftly swirled the red wine in his glass. He watched as the rich ruby liquid ran in tiny rivers down the inside and inexorably into the bowl.

"Not to your taste, sir?" the barman asked from across the gleaming wooden bar.

"It's fine," Ethan admitted, belatedly adding his thanks.

He continued to scan the crowd reflected in the mirror over the bar, and allowed his thoughts to wander. Rolled the truth around in his head that the life he'd lived since the accident had been based on untruths.

Looking back, he remembered that his father had been different after the crash. That bit more remote, that bit more stern and demanding of excellence in those around him. That bit less trusting. But once he'd recovered from his own injuries, Ethan, in his six-year-old mind, had rationalized that by believing his father was sad and lonely, just as he and Tamsyn were. So he'd tried his hardest, with everything, to be all his father demanded and more. And all for what? To discover that John Masters had been living a lie for the past twenty-five years and worse, had coerced everyone around him to do the same.

Even knowing it *had* been achieved, Ethan struggled to see how his father had carried it off. It was the stuff of soap operas, not his life. At least, not the life he'd thought he had.

He lifted the wine goblet and took a mouthful, letting the burst of berry and clove explode on his tongue before swallowing. Not bad, he conceded, but it stood in the shadow of his most recent international-award-winning Shiraz. Then the alcohol hit his stomach, reminding him he hadn't eaten since leaving The Masters, his family home and seat of their renowned winemaking business, early this morning.

"Deep in thought?"

The ultrafeminine voice caught his attention and he turned to take in the features of the slightly built blond-haired woman who'd inserted herself at the bar next to his chair. The butterfly. Up close he could see she was a little older than the average student here but she definitely didn't fit in with the corporate types, either. Her eyes were a bright, clear blue, her skin a honeyed light tan. Her eyebrows rose ever so slightly, awaiting his answer.

"Something like that," he responded.

"They say a problem shared is a problem halved," she offered with a welcoming smile. "Want to talk about it?"

Her lips glistened with the shimmer of a tinted gloss that perfectly complemented her skin. Her blond hair gleamed and fell in a short waterfall to shoulders exposed by the bright floral halter-necked dress that clung softly to her body. A bolt of sexual energy surged through him, but hard on its heels was a heavy dose of reality. Despite the fact he'd followed her in here, he wasn't the kind of guy who was into pub pickups. Hooking up with a stranger wasn't the answer to his problems. He wasn't ready for this—for her.

"No, thanks."

His response was more brusque than he'd intended. He was just about to add to it, to somehow soften what he'd said, when she gave him a thin smile, the warmth suddenly leaving her eyes as his "not interested" message got through loud and clear. He turned away slightly, feeling absurdly ashamed of himself, as she placed her order and waited for the barman to deliver it. He hadn't meant to be rude. After all, upon seeing her outside, hadn't he come in here seeking her?

Although she wasn't in his direct line of vision, he found himself acutely aware of her. Of her long, tapered fingers drumming on the wooden bar—her nails surprisingly short and practical—of her light summery fragrance wafting enticingly toward him in the air-conditioned environment. And particularly, of the gentle sway of her body in time to the beat of the music pumping from the bar's speakers. He should apologize, but as he turned to do so he discovered she'd already downed the shot she'd ordered and now threaded her way back through the crowd.

Relief that she'd moved on mingled with an odd sense of loss. Ethan took another sip of his wine and swiveled on his chair. Leaning back against the edge of the bar, he surveyed the writhing mass of people dancing on the floor. His eyes were immediately drawn to the blonde. She moved with inherent grace to the throb of the beat of the music and he was forced to acknowledge an answering throb in his own body. It had been too long since he'd relaxed and let his hair down. He should have encouraged her friendly overture rather than snubbed her. He scanned the room again before his eyes returned to her. He'd been too quick to turn away from her before and now he couldn't take his eyes off her.

A guy staggered up from a group of business types with a mounting collection of empties on their table, and made his way through the throng on the dance floor. He stopped behind the blonde woman, placing his hands on her hips and dancing suggestively behind her. Ethan felt a wave of possessive anger claw through him before pushing it back where it belonged. She wasn't his to worry about, he told himself. Even so, he still couldn't turn away—especially when she carefully placed her hands on her new dance partner's and took them from her body. Ethan stiffened on his chair. Having the other guy touch her was all well and good if she was happy with it, but when she so clearly wasn't...

The guy stumbled a bit, then righted himself only to grab at the woman's hand and turn her around to face him. He leaned forward to say something close to her ear. An expression of disgust slid across her face and she shook her head while trying to disengage his hold on her. This was wrong on so many levels it made Ethan's blood boil. *No* always meant no. Before he knew it, he was off his stool and edging his way through the dancers, his eyes firmly trained on one target and one target only.

"Sorry I'm late," he said, bending and placing a kiss on the startled woman's cheek. He turned slightly, placing his body firmly in front of her, and faced her wannabe beau. "She's with me, mate," he said, his stance and his expression saying in no uncertain terms that it was time for the other guy to back off.

To his relief the man gave him a drunken apologetic smile and returned to his table. Ethan turned back to the blonde.

"Are you okay?" he asked.

"You didn't need to do that. I can take care of myself, you know," she replied haughtily.

For some reason the thought of this svelte creature, who didn't even come up to his shoulder, "taking care of herself" made him laugh out loud. "That much was obvious," he said when he managed to get his mirth under control.

He was surprised when her face creased into a smile and she laughed along with him.

"I suppose I really should just say thank-you," she said, still smiling.

"You're welcome. You didn't look as if you were enjoying his company."

"No, you're right, I wasn't." She held out her hand. "I'm Isobel Fyfe."

"Ethan Masters."

He accepted her hand, instantly aware of the daintiness of hers in his much larger one. His fingers tightened reflexively as every one of his protective instincts roared to the forefront of his mind. He didn't let her go as he leaned forward slightly, his masculine bulk shielding her from those around them.

"Can I buy you a drink, or perhaps dinner somewhere else?" Ethan asked as he was jostled by the crowd. "It's a bit of a crush in here."

For a minute he thought she'd refuse but then she nodded.

"Dinner. Let me get my pack. The barman's holding it for me."

Ethan led her back toward the bar, her hand still in his. When she retrieved her large and well-worn backpack from behind the bar, Ethan automatically reached to relieve her of it as they made their way to the front door.

"It's okay," Isobel said. "I can manage. I'm used to it."

"Yes, but at least let me salve my male conscience by carrying it for you. I promise I won't lose it."

"Oh, well, when you put it like that." She smiled, handing the dusty pack, still with airline luggage tags attached, over to him. "Besides, it really doesn't match my shoes."

Ethan cast a glance at the high-heeled sandals she wore and had to agree. "Are you okay to walk in those or should we take a taxi?"

"Where were you thinking of going?"

He named a Greek restaurant farther down Rundle Street. "It's not far."

"Then let's walk," she said, slipping one small hand into the crook of his free arm. "It's a beautiful evening."

Ethan slung the pack over one shoulder, hardly caring for the creases it would generate in his Ralph Lauren Black Label suit.

"That wasn't your usual haunt, was it?" Isobel asked, nodding her head back toward the pub they'd just vacated.

"That obvious?" he asked with a smile.

For a moment he withstood her silent perusal as she eyed him carefully. The sense that she was checking him out in more ways than one made his blood begin to hum in his veins, sending warmth spreading out to his extremities.

"Yes," she answered succinctly.

Intrigued, he pressed her as to why.

"A few things," she said as they came to a stop at a street crossing and waited for their signal. "But mainly it's your demeanor. You've got this air about you. Some would say that it's probably wealth and privilege but I think there's more to it than that. You look like you aren't afraid of hard work." She took both of his hands in hers and turned them this way and that, examining them carefully before letting them go and tucking her hand back in the crook of his arm. "Yes, well tended but not in a prissy way. And yet there's an air of entitlement about you, or command, if you'd rather think of it that way. You're willing to work hard, but you're used to giving orders and having them immediately obeyed."

Ethan gave a short bark of laughter. "And you can tell all that just by looking at me?"

She shrugged—a delicate motion of her slender shoulders. "You asked," she replied simply. "Are we crossing?"

Her question reminded him that they were supposed to be going to dinner. He took a minute to clear his mind as they strolled across the intersection and down the sidewalk. How had this happened? he wondered, supremely conscious of her hand nestled at his elbow and the feminine sway of her hips as she walked along beside him. How had he gone from having a drink to unwind, to escorting a woman he'd only just met to dinner? How long had it been since he'd acted on impulse like this?

The answer to the last question was simple. Never.

Isobel felt the tensile strength of the forearm beneath her fingers and relished the tingle of anticipation it set up deep inside. The finely woven wool of Ethan's suit—she'd missed catching his last name in the noise back at the bar—was just a veneer to the man who wore it. Her senses fizzed with the same sense of excitement she got when she knew she'd captured a particularly good photo—that prickling spider-sense that she was on the verge of something greater than she'd experienced before. And, having made it a lifestyle choice to grab every moment and make it a worthwhile one, dinner with Ethan was just the ticket.

She wasn't the kind of girl who was free with her favors,

but she wasn't one to let the opportunity to spend a fun evening with an attractive man fall by the wayside, either.

Her instincts had told her he was straight up—that she had nothing to fear from him—and instinct had never let her down before. Besides, she had little reason to believe that anything would happen beyond an entertaining meal together. This guy was totally not her type. Too self-assured, too dominating and too darn good-looking for her equilibrium. Still, the evening promised to be interesting, if nothing else.

They arrived at the restaurant and she was immediately struck by the deference paid to him by the staff. After they were seated at the table, her pack secured safely on the floor between them, she couldn't keep the smile from her face.

"What's so funny?" he asked, reaching for his water glass and taking a long draw of the sparkling liquid. No mere tap water for him.

She dragged her gaze from the movement of the muscles in his tanned throat and reached for her own glass, lifting it to her lips.

"It's amazing. You just take it all for granted, don't you?" she eventually said.

The look of puzzlement that crossed his face, pulling his heavy dark brows together, was all the answer she needed.

"I don't follow."

"They treat you like royalty," she said with a small laugh. "And you don't even notice."

"I'm a regular, and I tip well," he replied, looking a bit put out.

"It wasn't a criticism," she said softly. "I'm sure they respect your patronage."

It only took a second for her double entendre to hit its mark, whereupon he surprised her by chuckling out loud.

"You don't pull your punches, do you?"

Isobel shrugged. "I believe in calling a spade a spade, even when it's a face card."

"So you gamble?" he probed.

"Only when I know I'm going to win," she conceded, looking down at her menu rather than meeting his dark-eyed stare across the table.

She thought for a minute of her last assignment. Her photography work gave her a chance to capture and highlight the best in people—and the worst. She was good enough to catch plenty of both, and not everyone was pleased with the results. Her most recent job had turned dangerous when the nation she'd been visiting had politely, but firmly, requested she remove herself from within their borders. It was clear that if she ignored them, their next request would not have been so civil.

On that particular assignment, she'd taken a gamble and she'd thrown in her hand before things got uglier. But she'd be heading back, as soon as she completed her next cookie-cutter job—one of the dull but easy assignments that gave her a measure of financial security. The new catalog shoot would be a walk in the park compared to her usual work and even though it wasn't as challenging on a social or emotional level as her preferred projects, it would ensure she had sufficient funds to head back to the war-torn country she'd just left to finish what she'd started.

"Do you win often?"

His voice was soft, like velvet, and she felt something deep inside her answer its challenge.

"As often as I can."

"It's hardly gambling when it's a sure thing," he commented before picking up his menu.

"You can't blame me for playing it safe." She nodded

toward the printed card in his hands. "What do you recommend?" she asked.

"Everything's good here but the lamb, in particular, is my favorite."

"Good. I'll have that then."

He closed his menu and put it down. "Just like that? You don't want another half an hour to peruse your choices and change your mind a half dozen times?"

"Why? Is that what you usually do?" she teased, knowing full well the answer would be an emphatic no.

He gave a slight shake of his head. "I prefer not to waste time. I'll order for us both."

"Thank you. I'd like that."

She watched carefully as he called the waiter over and placed their order, including a bottle of wine. Again the staff showed him that same respect they had before.

"You must tip *really* well," she mocked with a laugh. "I swear that guy was about to offer you his firstborn child."

"Hardly," Ethan responded drily before realizing that she was still teasing. "Ah, I see, you think it's fine to bait me? Okay then, I'll bite. Since you're clearly not in the habit of bribing waitstaff into providing good service, what do *you* do with your money?"

"My money?" Isobel pulled a face. "What I don't use for travel I try to use to help support worthy causes."

"Seriously?" His face pulled into a frown. "That's very philanthropic of you."

"I barely make a difference," she said, a note of sadness creeping into her voice as she remembered the helpless futility of some of the people she'd tried to help. "For myself, I've learned to need very little."

"What about when you grow older? How will you support yourself then?"

"I'll worry about that when it happens." His frown deepened, prompting her to ask, "You don't approve?"

"I didn't say that. Different strokes. I'm involved in a family business. We work together, socialize together—we're all striving for a common goal. With the business we have, we're looking forward to the future every day. I can't imagine just living in the day and not planning ahead. But then, as a family business, there are plenty of other peoples' futures at stake than just my own."

"I'm the only one affected by my decisions," she said simply, "which definitely has its advantages."

Ethan smiled back at her, and she knew that in some way, even if it was small, he probably envied her freedom. Most people did, but without realizing that it came with its own personal cost at the same time. Ethan clearly had a network of people to help and support him, while Isobel was very accustomed to being on her own.

She took advantage of the companionable silence between them to study him some more. In the subdued lighting of the restaurant, his lean features were all shadows and light. His nose a long straight patrician blade, his upper lip narrow but with a perfect bow to it, the lower lip fuller, enticing. His hair was worn short and controlled but she could detect the faintest of hints of curl in it and she wondered what he'd look like if he let it grow out a bit more, let himself look a little less disciplined and a lot more wild. Her fingers itched to reach for her camera in her pack and to shoot off a series of pictures of him.

The tingle that had started in her body earlier ramped up a notch, sending swirls of heat spooling through her belly and lower. The strong shadow on his jaw showed he was probably a two-shaves-a-day man, but somehow she knew she liked him better like this. Less polished, more primal. She squeezed her thighs together as a surge

of desire arrowed direct to her core, and in that moment
Isobel knew she was probably going to sleep with Ethan
whatever-his-last-name-was tonight and, more, that she
wanted to—very, very much.

Two

The food was delicious and she was glad she'd left Ethan to make their selections. She slipped up a little sauce from the edge of her plate with a finger and licked it off, her eyes closing briefly to enjoy the blissful flavor just that bit longer. When she opened them again, she caught Ethan staring at her. That earlier thrill of desire jolted through her again and she saw a flare of reciprocal interest light in his eyes.

What would he be like as a lover? she wondered as she broke eye contact and reached for her wineglass. He wasn't her usual type, which was probably a male version of herself—free-spirited, unfettered, casual. No, Ethan was definitely different. He exuded stability and strength, not to mention an unfair dose of sex appeal, and she found the combination fiercely compelling.

"Tell me about your travels," he said, leaning forward

to top up her wineglass with a little more of the very fine merlot they'd enjoyed with their meal.

So far they'd kept their conversation very general and superficial. So much so that neither of them really knew much about the other. Isobel preferred it that way. She didn't like to share too much of herself—at least not more than she was prepared to. She found so many people were critical of her attempts to expose some of the better-kept secrets regarding atrocities against children and families overseas. It was safer, she'd found, to be judicious with the information she shared.

She found it easy to fill the next hour with flip conversation of some of the funnier exploits she'd experienced. Ethan leaned back in his chair and laughed heartily at her recitation of her reaction to a giant centipede coming out of the hole in the ground she'd been using as a toilet during a trip through Nepal. Her own lips turned up in response to his unfettered joy. He had a great laugh, she decided. She liked it when a man could really give in to mirth. It was, in her mind, a good indicator of just how much he'd give in to anything else he was passionate about. Right now, she hoped that was her.

"Can't say I have anything in my experience to equal or better that," he said through his laughter. "And none of that puts you off or makes you want to take a more mainstream route?"

"No." She shook her head. "You don't really *see* the world as other people are forced to live it when you do that."

"Interesting choice of words."

"What?"

"Forced. Aren't most people living the life of their choice?"

She gave him a pitying smile. "You don't really believe that, do you?"

"I believe it's up to each individual to choose his own path."

"In a perfect world, maybe. Not everyone has the privilege of a perfect world."

Ethan considered her words before responding. "You're right. I'm being too general and thinking only in terms of here and my life, my choices." His face suddenly became serious and she felt his withdrawal as if it were a physical thing when in reality, he was no farther away from her than he'd been two seconds ago. "Even I don't have control over everything in my world."

He said it so bleakly, Isobel wondered for a moment what had happened to him that was so terrible. She reached across the table, pressing her fingertips lightly on the back of his hand where it rested on the pristine white tablecloth.

"I'm sorry," she said simply.

"Why sorry?"

"You strike me as the kind of guy who likes to be in charge of what happens."

"Yeah, I am," he admitted with a rueful smile. "And at least I can be in charge of how I react to what happens, right?"

They turned their conversation to more general topics after that, Isobel wringing more laughter from Ethan and reveling in the fact that she could. Seeing that glimpse of vulnerability in him had only made him even more attractive to her. It took a strong man to admit his weaknesses and she was hardwired to appreciate a strong man.

They'd been lingering over their coffee and dessert when she saw Ethan look at his watch. Around them, the restaurant had all but emptied.

"It's getting late," Ethan said. "Is there anywhere I can drop you off?"

"Oh, I'll be fine. I'll just check into the nearest hostel or hotel," she answered blithely, though she was admittedly a little sorry that their evening was drawing to a close.

The attraction she'd felt toward him all through the meal had only sharpened as she'd spent more time with him, and she wondered if perhaps he was too much of a gentleman to expect their evening together to lead to anything more. As much as she respected honor in a man, she wasn't feeling particularly honorable herself right now.

"You haven't booked anywhere?"

"No, I just flew in this afternoon. But it's no problem. There are a few places within walking distance of here, aren't there?" She could see Ethan bristle at the thought and she couldn't help the chuckle that bubbled from her at the expression on his face. "I can look after myself, you know."

"Like you did back at the pub?"

"I would have shaken him off eventually."

"Yes, it certainly looked that way." His delicious mouth firmed into a straight line.

"Hey, it's not a problem. I can get the restaurant to call me a cab if you're that worried. I only need a place for a night, anyway."

One night? One night of no questions, no answers. No recriminations. He would probably never see her again. One night of freedom, of passion. Ethan's mind expanded on the idea with the velocity of bush fire and with more than a hint of its searing heat, as well. He spoke before he could overthink the situation and talk himself out of the idea that had bloomed in his mind. If she went for it, all well and good. If not, no harm, no foul.

"Why not stay with me? I mean, I have an apartment

here in the city. There's more than enough room for you, as well."

To his surprise her smile widened.

"I'd like that." She hesitated a moment before continuing. "I'd like to stay *with* you tonight."

A knot of tension coiled tight in his gut. Did she mean what he thought she meant or had his simmering libido simply heard what it wanted to hear? In his whole life he'd never had a one-night stand—had considered them to be the mark of a person with little control, and even less respect for themselves. But his body burned in a way it had never burned before. Still, he felt obligated to be a gentleman about this.

"I have a couple of guest rooms. You can take your pick."

"Oh, I don't think that will be necessary," she replied softly. "Do you?"

He swallowed and shook his head. "Not if you're comfortable with that."

She laughed, the sound thrilling across his raw nerves like a soothing caress. "Oh, I expect to get really *un*comfortable, don't you? Come on, let's go."

Ethan was unused to someone else taking the lead but he couldn't deny the primal surge of attraction that flooded his body at her confidence. For once, the important decisions didn't lie solely with him. He didn't have to be the responsible one. He could just relax into doing what felt right. And this felt very, very right.

Without taking his eyes from her face, he gestured to the waitstaff for their bill. It felt like forever before the account was settled, with his usual generous tip added. Then he was hefting Isobel's pack up over his shoulder again. With his free hand he reached for her, threading their fingers together—the palm-to-palm contact hinting at the intimacy yet to come.

The short cab ride to his apartment building was executed in silence, the distance between them in the backseat of the cab miles rather than mere feet. But the instant they alighted, Ethan drew Isobel to him again. She looked up at the midrise apartment building and flicked him a wicked smile.

"Penthouse, right?"

He gave a small groan. "Guilty as charged."

"I love a view," she replied as they entered the building and took the elevator to the top floor. They entered a private foyer and Ethan watched as Isobel walked across the hardwood floors through a double-story-height room. She came to a halt in front of the wall of glass that looked out through the darkness, over Kurrangga Park and beyond.

"This is definitely a view," she said softly before turning around to face him. "But I think I like this view better."

She crossed the floor toward him as he placed her pack on the floor behind one of the oversize cream leather couches. As he straightened, her small hands slid around his waist beneath his jacket.

"Yeah, I definitely like this view better."

Isobel lifted herself on tiptoe and her lips caressed his ever so gently, like a butterfly kiss. As soft and near ephemeral as her touch was, the impact on his senses was so strong that it was as if someone had ignited every nerve in his body. He could feel her warmth even though she barely touched him. His nostrils flared as he breathed in the light essence of her scent. It wasn't enough. His hands reached for her, pulling her hard against him, absorbing her as her curves settled against the hard planes of his body. He lowered his head, watching as she lifted her face to him, her eyelids fluttering closed, her lips parting ever so slightly.

And then he kissed her as he'd been unconsciously dreaming of doing from the moment he'd first seen her. She was the perfect balance to him, light to his darkness, pliant to his inflexibility, warmth to the coldness that had settled deep inside him today. Resolutely he pushed all remembrance of what had led him to cross the same path as Isobel from his mind. She was here. He was here. That was the only thing that mattered in this moment.

Her lips were smooth and soft, her tongue a tiny dart that met his and tangled in a hot mess of need and desire. Her hands ripped at the buttons of his shirt, sending them bouncing onto the floor. She pushed the fabric open, baring his chest and belly to her touch. Her fingers spread across his skin, leaving a searing trail wherever she touched.

Ethan lifted his hands to her hair, letting the shoulder-length, silky strands run through his fingers as he reached to cup the back of her head and draw her even closer. He pressed his hips against her lower belly, instinctively seeking some relief for the increasing pressure that built in his groin. She pressed back and he groaned. He felt her hands skim across his belly to the belt of his trousers, where nimble fingers slid the leather free from its buckle, and began to unfasten his waistband. And then, mercifully, her hand was gripping him through his briefs, her fingers firm yet gentle at the same time. But he didn't want gentle. Not yet.

He ground against her hand and felt her answering response as she gripped him tighter. At the same time his fingers worked against the knot that bound the halter of her dress at the nape of her neck. The fabric finally gave way. Ethan pulled back from her slightly, allowing the top of her gown to slide down over her breasts, exposing them to his hungry gaze. Her nipples were a delectable, soft, peachy-pink, drawn into taut buds that begged for his mouth. He cupped one breast in his hand, rubbing the hard nub of her nipple with his thumb as he bent his head to its partner, drawing the tender flesh into his mouth and rasping its tip with his tongue.

A shudder passed through Isobel's body, a soft mew of pleasure emitting from between her lips. Ethan transferred his attention to her other breast, laving it with the same attention before he pulled back and bent slightly to slide one arm behind her knees and sweep her up into his arms. Her hands linked behind his neck and she pressed her lips against his chest as he strode to the master bedroom. Her teeth scraped across one nipple, making him almost stop in his tracks as a jolt of sheer lightning passed through his body. But he regained his focus, eventually shoving open the door that led into the bedroom where he slowly lowered Isobel to her feet.

She shimmied her dress over her hips, stepping out of the pool of fabric at her feet, even as she reached for him again. Dressed only in heels and the barest scrap of silk panties, she shoved his jacket off his shoulders and then dispensed with his shirt the same way. Ethan tugged down his pants and kicked off his shoes. He skimmed his socks off as he pushed his trousers away and reached for Isobel.

They tumbled to the bed together in a tangle of arms and legs, each trying desperately to get closer to the other, all the while touching and exploring the skin now exposed to them. He wasn't sure later how she engineered it, but she ended up straddling him, her legs trapping his thighs as she leaned down to trace his collarbone with the tip of her tongue before moving lower until she licked and nipped again at his nipples. His skin had never felt this sensitive, his responses this intense. He'd never felt so powerless, nor so empowered at the same time.

Even so, it wasn't in him to simply lie there, supine. Ethan stroked his fingertips over the tops of her thighs, then followed the line of her hip as it curved down along the edge of her panties and into the shadowed hollow of her core. He slid one finger under the flimsy covering, tugging the material aside and exposing her as a true blonde in the dimly lit room. She was wet and hot as he traced his finger around her moist flesh, dipping into her center. She ground against his hand, moaning her pleasure. He pressed his palm against her, even as he slid a second finger inside the scalding grip of her body. Again she pushed against him, her hips moving in a tight circle.

She ceased her exploration of his torso, sitting more upright, allowing him deeper access to her. He looked up at the vision of sheer femininity that hovered above him. Her eyes were open, staring straight into his, as if she could see into his very soul. Her breasts were small, perfect globes that shimmered in the half-light, her nipples drawn into concentrated buds. He stroked his fingers along her inner passage, pressed more firmly with his palm. Her body began to tremble, her stomach muscles—already flat and toned—tightening visibly as her whole body grew taut. And then he felt her crest the pinnacle of pleasure. Her inner muscles squeezing in paroxysms of satisfaction, her thighs shaking, a keening sound of fulfillment escaping from her, even though she had caught her lower lip between her teeth.

Ethan rose up and deftly moved her so she was beneath him, his hands now drawing her panties off her body, his fingers tracing the long, lean muscles of her legs. Once the lacy scrap was discarded, he slid her high-heeled sandals off her feet, massaging the instep of each foot before running his hands back up her legs again. The well-trimmed thatch of hair at the apex of her thighs glistened with the evidence of her gratification, and he nuzzled at the blond hair, inhaling the musky scent of her before exposing the swollen nub of flesh hidden inside. He traced a circle around the shining pink pearl with the tip of his tongue.

"Too soon," she protested weakly, her body still quivering with the aftereffects of her orgasm.

"Trust me, it's not soon enough," he argued, closing his mouth over the tumescent bead and gently scraping his teeth over its surface.

Isobel all but leaped off the bed, her hips surging upward in response to his action. Ethan swirled his tongue around her again, soothing her, before repeating the action with his teeth. She may have been in control of her last peak, but he most definitely would be driving her to her next. He increased the pressure of his tongue and began to suckle firmly. The next time he softly closed his teeth on her he felt her break, her body at first stretched as tight as a bow before the arrow of physical delight flew free, turning her muscles slack and supple beneath him.

He brushed his tongue over her again, then again more soothingly, until he finally withdrew from her and dragged himself up and over her.

"You okay?" he murmured, his hands now stroking her belly, tracing her rib cage and moving slowly to rest against one breast. Beneath his hand he could feel her heart hammering in her chest.

"Okay? Yeah, I think I'm just a bit more than okay," she said, smiling as she caught his face between her hands and kissed him. "But what about you?"

She flexed her pelvis against him.

"We're going to take care of that right now," he said. Supporting his weight on one arm, he reached with the other into the drawer of the nightstand.

He shook out the box of condoms he withdrew and grabbed one packet.

"Here, let me," Isobel insisted, taking the condom from his hand and tearing the foil open.

She slid the sheath from its confines and positioned it over the aching head of his erection before deftly sliding it over his length. It took almost every ounce of his control not to lose it as, once he was protected, she slipped her hand between them and positioned him at her entrance. She gasped as he probed her swollen, slick flesh, the sound vibrating through him as he fought to prolong this moment for as long as humanly possible.

Then, so slowly that it made his body shudder with the effort, he sank within her inviting depths. Her body gloved him, fitting so perfectly that he knew he would not be able to maintain this level of control for more than mere seconds. Bliss flooded him in an instant—potent and undeniable.

He moved within her, her hips rising to meet his every thrust, each one more powerful than the last, the rising pleasure becoming more exquisitely intense with each stroke. And then, he was there—sensation pulsating through his body and catapulting him into a place he'd never experienced so deeply before. He held her firmly to him, his forehead resting on hers, their rapid breaths mingling in the minute space between them. When he made to pull away, Isobel's arms closed around him.

"I'm too heavy for you," he protested as she squeezed tight.

"I like this," she replied as if the simplicity of the words themselves were fully sufficient.

He relaxed against her, and realized that maybe they were. He'd never felt the full acceptance of himself with another in the aftermath of lovemaking before. It had always been a release, often a deeply satisfying one, but never quite this sense of physical communion. He didn't know what to think of it, so he took what was—for him—a very novel approach. He decided not to think at all. Not just yet. As his heart rate slowed, he rolled slightly to one side, pulling her along with him.

Isobel reached up a finger to trace the line of his lips, her touch leaving a tingle of longing in its wake. He gave in and leaned into her to kiss her—not a kiss with the flaming sensuality they'd shared before, but one of quiet intimacy. Of thanks. He finally forced himself to break away and moved to rid himself of the condom, returning to the bed as quickly as he could and scooping her against him. Isobel tangled her legs in his and rested her head on his chest. For all that he barely knew her it felt almost frighteningly right.

One night, he reminded himself. That was all this was. Just one night.

Three

Isobel traced a circular pattern with her index finger on Ethan's chest. She'd been stunned by the force of their lovemaking, by their connection to one another. It almost seemed a shame that she'd be moving on to her next assignment tomorrow without ever seeing Ethan again, but she would live with that. She had to. It was the way she lived her life. Always fluid, always moving. Never staying still long enough to set down roots. It suited her.

And to her surprise, so had he.

She knew deep down that tonight had not been the type of thing a man like Ethan indulged in often, if at all. It piqued her curiosity. Why had he broken with what were probably very rigid personal boundaries to bring her home and share such profound intimacy? It was tempting to believe that it was just her influence that had him throwing caution to the wind, but she sensed that there was more to it than that. Her photographer's instinct always knew when there was more at play than what could be immediately seen. Before she knew it, the question slid from her lips.

"Why me, Ethan?"

"Huh?"

He sounded sleepy, as if she'd dragged him from that in-between place in the middle of consciousness and slumber.

"What happened to you today?" she asked.

He sucked in a deep breath and his arm tightened around her. "You don't want to hear about that."

"Try me," she coaxed. "You strike me as the kind of guy who doesn't usually share what troubles you. Maybe you should try it sometime, like now, with me."

She kept drawing the circles on his chest and waited in silence for him to make up his mind. She could almost hear the cogs turning in his brain as he weighed up the pros and cons of sharing with her. It never failed to surprise Isobel that people could share the most personal experiences together physically, yet reveal so little on an emotional level. Somehow it mattered to her to know why Ethan had overstepped his boundaries with her.

"I got some news today that I hadn't anticipated," he finally disclosed.

"Bad news?"

"Yes and no."

"It upset you," she stated firmly.

"Yeah, I don't know how to deal with it."

"It must have been really bad, then."

She felt him nod. "You could say that. My dad died recently and I've been going over his records. I found some payments that didn't marry up with the data I had before me, so I checked with the family accountant who referred me to our lawyer. That's where I went today. Basically I discovered that my father hid the truth about our mother from my sister and me. We were told she died twenty-five years ago, but she didn't. She left us and accepted his money to stay away."

"Oh, that's awful. You must have been devastated," Isobel whispered in shock.

She knew what it was like to find out a parent had been lying to you. It was the deepest kind of betrayal.

"I don't understand why he did it and now I can't ask him, either."

Tension radiated from his body as the frustration he'd been feeling wound tight inside of him.

"Maybe he just wanted to protect you and your sister. If it happened twenty-five years ago then you can't have been all that old," she said, trying to soothe him.

"I was six, my sister only three. I would have had some understanding of his decision not to tell us then, if my father had bothered to tell me the truth later, when I was an adult. It's not as if he didn't have ample opportunity. Even after he died, there was no letter, nothing in his will to let me know the truth. If I hadn't started asking questions about the payments, I never would have known."

The bitterness in his voice hung in the air.

Isobel sighed. "It isn't easy to understand the choices our parents make." That much, she knew from personal experience. "Usually, I guess they think they're protecting us."

"Why would I need to be protected from the truth? Don't I deserve to know why he thought my sister and I would be better off without our mother in our lives?"

"Maybe it wasn't as clear-cut as that."

Ethan shook his head. "It must have been. Otherwise, he wouldn't have been able to get the rest of our family to support him in his lie. My aunt and my uncle and his wife, they all knew the truth. They've all kept the secret for all these years."

"Are they still alive?"

"Yeah, we all live on the family property. We see each other pretty much every day."

"Then maybe you can find out from them," she suggested. "Whatever the outcome, though, Ethan, there's no point in holding a grudge against a dead man. Right or wrong, your father made his decisions. They can't be undone or the past changed. The only thing you can do is move forward."

"Is that what you do?" he asked. "Move forward and not ask questions?"

She smiled and lifted her head and met his serious dark brown gaze. "Except for right now, yeah, something like that. It saves on baggage."

Ethan shook his head slightly. "I can't imagine living like that."

Isobel shrugged. "It's not for everyone. Certainly not for someone like your father, for example. For whatever reason, he kept those payments going for years, got your whole family involved, with the idea that he was protecting you and your sister. I imagine you're probably very much like he was. Strong." She coasted her fingertips over his shoulders and down his arm. "Intelligent." She ran her fingers back up his arm and lightly touched his forehead. "And protective." Her fingertips traveled back down to his chest and she rested her full palm against it. "Those are the qualities about your father you should remember him by. And how much he must have loved you."

Ethan remained silent for a while before speaking. "You have an interesting insight for someone who never met my father and who never met me before tonight."

"You think I'm being presumptuous, offering you my opinion?"

"No, not that. If anything, you probably described my

father to a tee. I suppose that coming to terms with everything, losing him as suddenly as we did, I had briefly lost sight of that. I still want to know why he never told me about our mother, though."

"Is tomorrow soon enough for that?" Isobel asked, raising onto her knees and straddling him as she'd done earlier. "Because I think, for now, it might be fun to distract you with other things."

Four

Isobel woke as the sun was beginning to cast a corona around the edges of the heavy floor-length drapes at the window. For a moment she was disoriented, but soon remembrance flooded her mind. She lay motionless next to Ethan's sleeping body, listening to his steady breathing, reveling in the warmth that radiated from him. Wow, she thought, that had been quite a night. Who would have thought that Mr. Buttoned-Up would be quite so skilled in the bedroom? She smiled to herself. It was true what they said. It was the quiet ones you had to watch.

Her body still tingled and she felt wonderfully alive. Last night had been special. Very special. She turned her head on the pillow and looked at Ethan in the half light. His beard had grown, dusting his jaw with an even darker haze than had been apparent at dinner. That, and his mussed-up hair, made him look more untamed and approachable than he'd been before. It was as if he was two people. A public, reserved Ethan and a private one. She liked that she'd gotten a chance to spend time with both.

Her fingers itched to reach out and touch him. To awaken him both mentally and physically. But caution stilled her hand. If she was going to leave, best to leave now, while he was still sleeping. That way, they could avoid the awkward goodbye that would come after she told him she'd rather not keep in touch. She wasn't prepared to invest time into any type of commitment. It wasn't her way. And this guy, well, he had commitment written all over him. In fact, she didn't doubt that she'd been an aberration for him.

She slid carefully from the bed and found her dress and shoes on the floor at the end of the bed. Her panties were a lost cause, she decided, after silently scanning the carpet for a minute. Besides, she had clean pairs in her pack. Giving a mental shrug, she held her things to her and carefully made her way to the door, thanking the efficiency of modern maintenance that the door opened and closed silently, allowing her to exit the bedroom without making a sound.

In the main room she located her pack behind the sofa where Ethan had left it last night and quickly got dressed. She'd give just about anything for a hot shower and a toothbrush right now, but she didn't want the sound of running water to wake Ethan. Now that she'd made her decision to cut and run, she didn't want anything to stand in her way. Not even the man who'd ensured she'd enjoyed what had unarguably been the best sex of her entire life.

Her inner muscles clenched on the memory of the pleasure he'd wrung from her. No hit and miss with him. She smiled. No, he was hit after hit every time. A girl could get addicted to that, could want to hang around for more of the same. She reminded herself that she wasn't the hanging-around type. Not for any reason, and certainly not for a man. She was a wanderer through and through, with little to call her own aside from what she could carry in her pack.

Ethan had talked about a family business, relatives that he worked with and spent time with every day. She couldn't imagine an existence more different from her own. No, there was no room for commitment in her life, and no place for some as impermanent as her in his.

Isobel threaded the straps of her shoes through the fingers of one hand while hoisting her pack over one shoulder with the other. She turned to blow a silent kiss in the direction of Ethan's bedroom. It had certainly been fun while it lasted.

In the elevator on the way to the ground floor, Isobel slid her sandals onto her feet and smoothed her dress, thanking the good sense she'd learned years ago to only purchase non-crush fabrics. Sometimes it cost a little more, but it was worth it when you lived a transitory life out of a backpack.

The air had a definite autumnal chill to it when she exited the massive glazed doors of the apartment building and she hesitated under the portico, deciding where she should head to next.

She really needed to find somewhere inexpensive to check into so she could shower and change and get her professional head back on her shoulders. Last night had been a sinfully satisfying deviation from her usual behavior but the sooner she put it behind her, the better. Question was, how was she to do that? She waited in the cool morning air for a few minutes and then, as luck would have it, a taxi pulled to the curb to drop off a passenger. Someone returning from overseas, judging by the amount of luggage the driver hefted from the trunk of the car. As he started to get back in, Isobel stepped forward.

"Excuse me, is there any chance you could take me to a low-price hotel near here?"

"Sure, love. Hop in."

Thanking her lucky stars, Isobel pushed her pack into the backseat and followed it onto the worn upholstery. As the car pulled away, though, she wondered what might have happened if, instead of slinking away, she'd stayed to waken Ethan. Where could they have gone from last night? That they would have made love again was in no doubt. In fact, they could have skipped the potential for morning-after awkwardness and worked their way straight through to afternoon delight.

No, she told herself sternly, forcing her head to remain resolutely facing forward. As good as their night together had been, she had to remember her motto, her very code for living. *Never look back.*

Besides, she had work to do that would have drawn her out of town soon, anyway. A job that was a cakewalk when it came to it, but that would bring in a tidy paycheck. It was these safe, easy glamour jobs that gave her some much-needed rest after a more trying assignment, and paid enough to subsidize the side of her work that was really important.

She'd allowed herself a month to get the project completed to both her and her client's satisfaction. One month to recoup funds, to rest and recharge, and then she was heading back to the African continent. Back to what she did best and what spoke to her heart. What she earned in the next few weeks would grease the palms necessary to get her exactly where she needed to be to take the pictures she needed to take.

But even as the tires on the taxi ate the kilometers putting space between her and Ethan, she still felt that tug— that desire to turn back. To explore the vulnerability that

lay beneath the face Ethan presented to the world at large.
To revel in the strength and capability he exuded. The guy
was addictive. Dangerously addictive. It was just as well
she'd never see him again because deep down she knew
he had the power to make her want to stay with him longer than a night and she couldn't do that.

No, she'd never do that.

Ethan stretched against the fine cotton of the bedsheets
and reached beside him for Isobel's sleeping form, but his
hand came up empty. In fact, the room itself held an emptiness that left him in no doubt that she'd moved on.

Conflicting thoughts plagued him as he rolled out of bed
and walked naked into the main living area of the apartment, just to confirm she had indeed gone. Relief that they
didn't have to face any stilted morning-after discussion,
tempered with a deep regret that they couldn't start the
day the way they'd finished last night, warred within him.

Relief won out. Especially in light of the discussion
they'd had after the first time they'd made love. What on
earth had possessed him to open up in such detail to an
absolute stranger? He hadn't even told his sister the news.
In fact, he didn't even know if he *would* tell her.

Wasn't it far better that Tamsyn remember their dad the
way he'd have wanted to be remembered—not as a man
who'd deliberately altered their family history without so
much as an explanation left behind when he died? Didn't
she deserve at least that? Ethan didn't even want to con-
template what it would do to Tamsyn to learn their mother
had willingly abandoned them. How it would destabilize
the world they'd grown up in.

God, it was all such a mess. No less so than it had been
yesterday but, he had to admit as he walked back into the
bedroom and headed for a shower, at least he himself felt

a little better about it. Somehow, Isobel Fyfe had woven her magic around him from the minute he'd seen her. Just that one chance glimpse of her before she entered the pub, like a butterfly alighting on a leaf, and his day had taken a decided turn for the better. He turned on the shower and stepped in before the water could come up to temperature, yet even the multijet sprays couldn't shake the lingering sensation of her touch from his body, or his mind. Somehow, she'd inveigled her way into his thoughts so thoroughly, and in so short a time, that he couldn't fully dislodge her.

She wasn't his type, he reminded himself. She was only a one-night stand, by her own choice. He hadn't kicked her out—she was the one who had left. Their night together had satisfied both of them, and then she had moved on. It was for the best. It was what he'd wanted, too, after all. The prospect of a single night of no-consequence pleasure with a stranger was the only reason he'd invited her back to the apartment. He never expected to see her again. Yet he could still remember the precise pitch of her laugh, the softness of her voice, the warmth of her breath on his skin, the texture of her tongue as it—

Ethan switched the mixer to cold. This wasn't getting him anywhere but uncomfortable. No, it was best that she'd gone as she had—leaving no trace other than the lingering scent of her fragrance on his bedsheets and the indelible imprint she'd left on his mind. The bedsheets would be taken care of by housekeeping, his mind he could take care of himself. He just needed to change his focus.

Later, as he got ready to head home, back to his work at the winery, he told himself he was succeeding. They couldn't have taken things any further than they had, even if they'd both been interested in doing so. She was completely disconnected from the things that formed the cornerstones of his world. She was a transitory creature of light and laughter—charming, but unreliable. He was stable, grounded in his work and his family. The people in his life depended on him. He needed to be able to depend on them, as well.

He'd needed distracting last night and she'd definitely been quite the distraction.

It was with a satisfied smile on his face that he let himself out of the apartment half an hour later and took the elevator to the basement-level parking. The Isobel Fyfes of this world were good for a fling, and they'd enjoyed a mutually pleasurable one at that, however, she couldn't be further from his idea of a forever woman in his life if she'd actively been trying.

No, it was women like Shanal Peat, one of his old university friends who more closely fit that bill. She was serious and clever and, with her mixed Indian and Australian heritage, exquisitely beautiful. They were already close friends. She'd be a far better life mate for a man like Ethan than Isobel could ever be, plus, with her Ph.D. in viticulture, she'd be a brilliant asset to The Masters winery and vineyard. He could see her fitting in well with his family, with her gentle, steady demeanor. She'd understand and respect the generations of tradition that went into their family vineyard, and would slide seamlessly into their lives and work with no confusion or upheaval.

It would be a mistake to even consider someone more bold, more unexpected and spontaneous. Women like that added excitement to life, but they added chaos, as well. No, a woman like Shanal was exactly what he needed. They were a melding of minds and personalities that could only succeed.

Ethan got into his 5-series BMW and headed out the basement and into the glorious sunshine of another beautiful Adelaide autumn morning. This business with his parents was just a minor glitch. He could take care of it later. And, he wagered, as long as the payments to Ellen Masters continued unabated, he had no reason to worry about her suddenly returning and reasserting her parental rights. The secret could remain a secret a while longer. There was no need for his aunts and uncle to know he was aware of the truth—or for his sister to know anything about the matter at all.

By the time he cruised through the gates of The Masters and past the cellar door tasting room and point of sale, it was late morning. He turned down the private road that led to the main house and pulled his car to a halt outside. As he got out of the car, he took a moment to breathe in the scent of the air and fill his lungs with it.

Home. There was nothing quite like it. His eyes drifted to the top of the ridge where the shell of his family's old home, Master's Rise, destroyed by bush fire more than thirty years ago, still stood. The stone-wall construction of the late-nineteenth-century building had withstood the voraciously hungry flames that had systematically consumed most of the property, and proved too solid to be economically torn down. Its profile endured as a constant reminder of what could be lost, while the lands that roamed beneath it continued as proof of what could be achieved in the face of disaster.

Ethan looked around at what his family had rebuilt in his father's lifetime. The large double-storied home that housed most of the family under its roof, the vineyards stretching across the valley and up the hill, the winery, which consumed Ethan's time and expertise and challenged him in all ways to constantly do better. Yeah, it was good to be home and even better to have this all to come home to.

A movement on the path from one of the luxury cottages, which provided accommodation for guests, caught his attention. Tamsyn, his sister, ran that side of the business, and had probably just finished the final inspection of the cabin for a guest before walking back toward the house.

"Good morning," she said with a smile as she drew nearer. She gave an exaggerated look at her watch. "Or should I say, afternoon?"

He smiled in return. "It's still morning," he confirmed.

"Did you have a good night in town?" she inquired innocently, although the sparkle in her eyes told him she was delving for more information.

"Yeah, thanks," he replied, deliberately vague.

Tamsyn sighed. "No gossip?"

"Since when have I been the subject of gossip?"

"You know what I mean," she said on a huff of disappointment. "You need to get a life, Ethan. Sometimes you're just too absorbed in this place."

He looked at her this time, really looked. There was a note in her voice that implied dissatisfaction in her world, something he'd never heard from her before.

"Is everything okay, Tam?"

She pasted on a broad smile. "Of course. Why wouldn't it be, right? By the way, are you going to be at dinner this evening? I have the new photographer for the catalog shoot arriving later this afternoon and I'd like you to meet—"

"Sure, I'll be there," he interrupted. "Same time, same place," he said with a wink.

It was a family joke. Whichever family members were in residence usually met for predinner drinks in the main salon before dining together. It was a good way to stay in touch, although he knew that some people found it a bit old-fashioned. Personally, he liked that some traditions remained the same, and there was always the option of cooking for yourself—something he was generally loath to do. It would be tough, though, facing his aunts and his uncle. Looking them in the eye and knowing they had conspired to keep a secret from Tamsyn and him for all this time. Did they not wonder, now John Masters was dead, if the truth would come out? Well, Ethan certainly wouldn't be throwing it into the conversational pot tonight. He still needed time to come to terms with it himself.

He continued. "How's the wedding business going?"

"Mine, or for here?"

As part of her work in running the accommodation side at The Masters, Tamsyn also oversaw special events—business retreats and the like. Since her engagement to Trent Mayweather just over a year ago, she had happily expanded into coordinating small, but exclusive, wedding packages at the property.

"Either. Both." Ethan shrugged.

"Fine. The latest bridezilla would seem to finally be appeased by the fact that, since harvest is well and truly under way, we will not have green vines flush with grapes for her favored photo shoot, so overall things are looking good. And since Trent and I have yet to set a date, there's no business to worry about there," she replied airily.

Still no date. Despite her determined attempt to sound flip about the issue, Ethan sensed there was an underlying hint of frustration in her voice. Before he could press her further, Tamsyn changed the subject.

"Did you manage to get everything done that you needed to in the city?"

A shadow passed over him and he suppressed a small shiver. Tam had enough on her plate right now without more stress. He was glad he'd decided not to share his father's secret with her yet.

"It's all the same old, same old."

Tamsyn began to speak but the cell phone in her hand began to chime the wedding march. "Uh-oh, bridezilla again. I need to take this. Talk later?"

Ethan gave her a nod and watched as she pasted on a smile while she answered the call and slowly walked toward the house. She did that a lot lately, he realized. Fake smiled, faked being happy. He'd put it down to grief over their father's sudden death, but he couldn't help but wonder if there wasn't more to it. Trent appeared to have offered her precious little support to date. Sure, the guy was busy at his inner-city law practice, but there were times when loved ones came first. Were things not entirely right in their relationship? He made a mental note to dig a little deeper next time he and Tam were alone together, but for now he had other demands on his time. Work demands that he should have been here earlier to attend to…if he hadn't been so willingly distracted last night.

Ethan entered the salon later that evening, satisfied he'd put in a good afternoon's work at the winery. Fermentation had begun on the first of the season's harvests and he had high hopes for the new wine. As he walked into the room, he scanned those already there. His aunt Cynthia reigned with her usual regal decorum, his uncle Edward stood head to head with his wife, Marianne, in quiet discussion.

Looking at them, no one would have suspected they'd colluded with their brother, John, to hide the truth about Ethan and Tamsyn's mother.

Still, in this family, blood ran deep and thick and, up until his death, John had been very much the patriarch whose word was final. With a little more distance from the revelation, Ethan found himself more willing to forgive his relatives for falling in line with his father's wishes. If whatever he'd decreed had been seen to be in the best interests of the family and the business, it would have been adhered to. No matter the cost.

Ethan joined his cousins, two of Edward's three adult children, Cade and Cathleen, who ran the cellar door, tasting room and café operation at the property.

"Busy day?" he asked them after he'd poured himself a glass of Shiraz.

"Busloads today," Cathleen commented ruefully. "The poor kitchen staff was flat out with washing dishes by hand after the dishwasher broke down, and there's still tomorrow's usual Sunday crowd to come. I've called in a couple of casuals to help out."

"That's good. So, are you still wanting to expand to include dinners with the café menu?" Ethan asked.

"Of course," Cade confirmed. "The figures are looking good for the expansion. Demand is already there. Besides, with Tamsyn's wedding side of things becoming more popular, it makes sense to ride on her coattails. After attending a wedding here, there've been plenty of guests who have wanted to come back for an evening meal at another time."

Ethan nodded. It was surprising how, in such a short period of time, the family business had expanded from purely being a vineyard and winery to what was now far more diverse than what their grandparents, or even their parents, had ever imagined. Cade and Cathleen's older brother, Raif, worked the viticulture side of The Masters with his father.

"Did you hear that Tamsyn managed to secure IF Photography for the new catalogs?" Cathleen interrupted his thoughts. "Our chef is beside himself with glee and can't wait for her to start."

"Tam mentioned something about a photographer," Ethan said absently. Tamsyn hadn't turned up yet tonight. He hoped she was okay.

"*Award-winning* photographer. She's from New Zealand, apparently, but travels worldwide," Cathleen corrected excitedly. "We're lucky to get her at all but to have her here for a month doing all aspects of The Masters is amazing. The new catalogs and web photos will be fantastic."

"Well, they do have great material to work with," Ethan said with a wink. "Speaking of Tam, do you know where she is tonight? I thought she'd be here by—"

A frisson of awareness traced a ghostly fingertip down the back of Ethan's neck.

"She's just arrived," Cathleen said, gesturing toward the entrance to the salon. "Oh, and look who's with her! She must be the photographer. Let's go and say hi."

Ethan stiffened and all his senses went on alert as Cade and Cathleen went over to greet the newcomers. IF Photography. *IF*. The initials trickled through his mind coming to one conclusion. Isobel Fyfe.

Surely not.

He turned and faced his sister and her guest and felt the blood drain from his head in shock as he recognized the angel-haired woman at his sister's side.

Five

Isobel saw the exact moment Ethan registered her presence and noted as, in equal measures, shock and then anger flooded his features. Tamsyn was happily oblivious to Ethan's rising fury as she introduced Isobel to Cade and Cathleen and then to the others in the room, working in a circle until they ended up in front of Ethan.

Masters. So that was his surname. A shame she hadn't paid more notice at the time, Isobel thought with an inward cringe. It would certainly have avoided this predicament. Clearly, he thought she knew, and was not happy that she'd kept their upcoming encounter a secret.

Every line in Ethan's body broadcast his displeasure at her appearance and his brows pulled together in a forbidding line.

"Ethan, this is Isobel Fyfe, the photographer I was telling you about. Isobel, this is my big brother, Ethan. Don't pay too much attention to him. His bark is always way worse than his bite."

Isobel felt her cheeks flame with color. She knew exactly what Ethan's bite was like. In fact, she still had a few faint marks on her body here and there to prove it. She extended her hand and waited for Ethan to observe the proprieties.

"Ms. Fyfe," he said stiffly, finally extending his hands and briefly clasping hers.

As brief as the contact was, she knew he felt the same flare of physical reaction she did. His eyes flamed ever so briefly before resuming their cold appraisal of her.

"Please, call me Isobel," she said with a smile that felt artificial on her lips. "I prefer not to stand on formality."

"And you must call him Ethan," Tamsyn said. "We're all on first-name terms here."

Isobel cast a look at Ethan, a little unnerved by the intensity of his glare. It made a small wave of anger rise inside her. He had no need to be so angry or distant. She hadn't kept anything from him deliberately—she honestly hadn't realized their paths would cross again. And was it so terrible that they had? Did he think she was the type to kiss and tell? It wasn't like she was about to share intimate details of his sexual prowess with the people in the room with them. Nor was she likely to bring up the matters he shared with her about his parents. His bristling attitude was offensive and she didn't hesitate to turn away from him when Tamsyn drew her attention to another part of the room.

She could feel his eyes boring in her back as they walked away and it raised her ire another notch. How dare he treat her that way? Sure, they'd neither of them expected to see one another again but she'd never have anticipated him being so...so distant. Jerk.

Unbidden, the shaded image of him over her body, slowly entering her, driving her to another glorious peak of satisfaction, speared through her mind. She drew in a sharp breath as her body gave a sudden pulse of remembered pleasure.

"Are you okay?" Tamsyn asked. "I'm sorry about Ethan. He's usually far more friendly. I think there's something bothering him at the moment and, knowing him, we won't hear about it until he's sorted it all out himself." She gave a little embarrassed laugh.

"I'm fine, really," Isobel hastened to reassure her. What had happened between her and Ethan was between the two of them only, and by the looks of things, Ethan was suffering from an overabundant dose of regret. Well, that was his problem, Isobel decided. She was here to do a job and that's exactly what she was going to do.

She focused her attention back to Tamsyn. "Tell me about your cousins—Raif, Cade and Cathleen. Am I right? Aren't those the names of the Calvert children in *Gone with the Wind?*"

Tamsyn laughed. "Yeah, Aunt Marianne is a big Margaret Mitchell fan."

All through the evening and even during dinner she could still feel Ethan watching her, but she did her best to ignore him. They were seated at opposite ends of the long and impeccably set dining table and it took next to no effort to keep her own gaze riveted to the other family members around her. She thought she had everyone pegged so far.

Cynthia was very much in charge of the household. A beautiful woman, but with a hardness about her mouth and eyes that gave fair warning that she had very high expectations of those around her. She'd make an interesting photographic study. Edward and his wife appeared to be close, and generally friendlier than Cynthia. Isobel wondered how Ethan and Tamsyn's father must have fit into all of this. She assumed he would have been the eldest of the family, much as Ethan was amongst his cousins.

The Masters family made for interesting watching, that was for sure. All attractive in their own ways, and each with very clearly defined personalities and yet close-knit at the same time. It was a fascinating dynamic from the point of view of someone who had grown up as an only child and without extended family. A long-hidden part of her felt a deep twinge of envy at the easy way they all took one another's presence in each other's lives for granted, but she suppressed it almost as swiftly as it surfaced.

Never look back.

It was later, as the evening was drawing to an end and only a few remained at the table drinking coffee and lingering over their desserts, that she proffered her thanks for the evening and rose from the table. To her surprise, Ethan rose, too.

"I'll see Isobel to her accommodation," he said firmly, his hand squeezing Tamsyn's shoulder gently and keeping her in her seat as she made to rise with them. "You go on up and have an early night."

"If you're sure?" Tamsyn said, looking up at her brother and then across at Isobel.

"I can make my own way," Isobel said quickly. "The path is well lit and it's a beautiful evening."

"I wouldn't think of letting you walk back alone on your first night," Ethan said smoothly, closing the distance between them and gesturing to the French doors that led outside to the massive wraparound decking.

Once they were a short distance from the house Ethan drew to a halt.

"What are you playing at?" he asked in a steely tone.

"Playing?"

"Why didn't you tell me last night that you were coming here?"

Isobel gave a humorless laugh. "Because I didn't know this was your home. I didn't catch your surname over the noise in the bar and I really didn't think it mattered enough to ask."

"It matters. I want you to leave. Make up some excuse in the morning and just go. I'll cover your costs."

"Wow, that's good of you, especially since you probably have no idea of what I charge," Isobel said with as much sarcasm as she could muster. "But I think you're forgetting something. I am a professional and I've entered into a contract with The Masters to provide my services. That's exactly what I'm going to do."

"I'm sure there's an out clause in there somewhere. Look, I'll even pay a premium on top of your fee."

"What makes you think I'm so desperate for money that I'd do what you're asking?"

"For goodness' sake, you live out of a backpack and, by your own admission last night, you don't *own* anything of real value. Of course you want the money."

Her pride stung at his arrogance. Was this the real Ethan Masters? How could he be so different from the man she'd spent last night with?

"Look, I'm more than happy to stay out of your way but my contract is with Tamsyn and her marketing division, and I always honor my contracts."

He took a step closer and instantly her senses were flooded with the warmth emanating from his body, and the discreet lightly wooded scent he wore. She inhaled it without thinking and her body went on full alert—her nipples tightening, her breasts feeling full and heavy and aching for his touch. Heat gathered low down in her body.

God, even at his condescending worst she was attracted to him. How pathetic was that?

"But that's part of the problem, isn't it, Isobel? You won't be able to stay out of my way—and more than that, you won't be able to stay out of Tamsyn's way."

She had been turned away from him slightly, refusing to meet his dark eyes as she stared at a point in the fragrant garden just beyond them, but her surprise at this turned her eyes back to lock with his.

"What's wrong with me interacting with Tamsyn? You're a grown man—even if she finds out that we spent the night together, why would she care?"

"I'm not worried about that, I'm worried about you sharing my confidences in you with Tamsyn."

Again she felt the stinging barbs of his words. Isobel drew in a steadying breath and faced him full on.

"Ah, so you haven't told your sister yet? Don't you think you ought to? She deserves to know."

"That's for me to decide. Look, I barely know you, I don't know if I can trust you, or if I even want to."

"Well, that's just a risk you're going to have to take, isn't it?"

She turned and stepped away, determined that was the end of their conversation, but warm fingers caught at her hand and tugged her back toward him. Fiery tendrils of desire wound their way through her body.

"I'm warning you, Isobel. I'm not a man to be tangled with. Do not disclose any of what I told you to my sister."

Isobel yanked her hand loose, absently rubbing it with her other hand in a vain attempt to wipe away the lingering sensation of his touch.

"And I'm not the kind of woman who responds well to orders," she hissed back at him. "Don't worry—I already regret meeting you. *Tangling* with you again, as you so eloquently put it, is the last thing on my mind."

She stalked away from him, her entire body vibrating with anger. How dare he treat her this way? If it wasn't such a matter of principle for her to never walk away from a job, she'd have told him exactly, and in explicit detail, where he could shove his money and his stupid family secrets. Isobel's eyes burned. To her shock she realized she was crying. She never cried. Tears of anger, that's all they were, nothing more. She swiped at the moisture on her cheeks and silently vowed not to let Ethan Masters get under her skin again for the duration of her stay here. In any way, shape or form.

Ethan watched Isobel until she reached the cottage she'd been assigned. He flinched as he heard the heavy wooden front door slam closed. It would seem he'd managed to get his point across—rather more forcefully than he'd intended. He shook his head. In his shock at seeing her here tonight, in his home, he'd allowed anger to cloud his decisions, to direct his behavior. He'd lacked his usual level of control. And it hadn't just been because he worried about her spilling secrets. No, it was because in spite of his concerns, in spite of the very real damage she could do to his family, he still couldn't stop himself from being damnably drawn to her. She did that to him.

He turned and walked slowly toward the main house. His direct approach to Isobel had been clumsy, but he still had another option up his sleeve to get her to leave. Isobel had insisted her contract was with Tamsyn—that meant Tamsyn could withdraw it. He looked up to the second-story windows that he knew were his sister's. The lights were still on. He let go a short sigh of relief. Good, he could deal with this tonight rather than wait until morning.

Ethan let himself into the house and headed for the main stairs. In no time his knuckles rapped out a gentle tattoo on Tamsyn's door.

"Ethan?" she said from inside.

"Yeah, got a minute?"

"Sure, come in."

He let himself into the room and closed the door behind him. His sister was curled up on the small sofa in front of an empty fireplace. It wouldn't be long before the small cavern would be glowing with the cheerful light of a fire as autumn slowly gave way to winter, but today its emptiness seemed sad and lonely.

"Did you see Isobel to the cottage okay?" Tamsyn asked, putting down the book she'd been reading onto a side table.

"I did, and she's what I want to talk to you about."

"Really?" An expression of interest flickered across his sister's features. "What do you want to know?"

Ethan rested one hand on the polished wooden mantel and chose his next words carefully.

"How much do you know about Isobel Fyfe?"

"What I've heard by referral mostly, and from her website. Why? Are you worried about something? Don't you think she's capable of doing the job?"

"I don't think she's right for the job, to be honest. Can we break the contract, Tam?"

Tamsyn sat upright and looked at him in surprise. "Break the contract? Why?"

"I'd rather we use someone else," he said bluntly.

"Seriously, Ethan, without a very good reason I'm not going to break the contract with Isobel. She came very highly recommended and her portfolio is extensive. We were lucky to get her as much of her work is done overseas, and she's only in Australia for a month. What have you got against her?"

"I'd prefer not to say."

This was more difficult than he'd thought. Normally, Tamsyn was only too happy to acquiesce to his suggestions but in this instance, of all instances, she'd decided to be stubborn.

"Well, like I said before, unless you can give me a good reason, she's staying."

What reason could he give his sister? That, because of his carelessness, Isobel held a secret that could rock the foundations of Tamsyn's world? That she held the key to unlocking a potential world of hurt and unanswerable questions?

Tamsyn's eyes, so like his own, bored into him as he remained silent. He saw the exact second an idea occurred to her.

"You're attracted to her, aren't you?" Tamsyn could be equally as blunt as him.

"That's not the point," he said, unable to straight out lie to her and deny her observation.

Tamsyn smiled. "What are you afraid of, Ethan? Following your heart?"

"There's no danger of my heart being involved," he said firmly. "Besides, you know I plan to marry Shanal one day."

Tamsyn snorted in an unladylike fashion. "Look, I love Shanal, she's a great friend but there's no spark between you. Why are you afraid of exploring something with someone who doesn't come in a paint-by-numbers relationship?"

Paint by numbers? Was that what she thought of his friendship with Shanal? Just because he considered a relationship between them rationally, evaluating the different traits and compatibilities they'd bring to a marriage rather than getting swept away in meaningless passion? What was wrong with that?

And as to exploring "something" with Isobel, he'd already been there. Talk about getting swept away… His fists clenched involuntarily as his body was flooded with remembrance of what they'd been doing with one another only twenty-four hours ago. He tamped the wayward sensation down by sheer force of will.

"There's no shame in leading with your head rather than your heart, Tam."

"That's not my point," Tamsyn said, getting up from the sofa and coming to stand in front of him. "You're my brother and I love you, Ethan. But sometimes you infuriate me, especially when you are hell-bent on controlling everything around you. Some things are not meant to be controlled."

"Look, I didn't come in here for a discussion about my love life. I came to talk about Isobel Fyfe's unsuitability."

To his surprise, Tamsyn laughed out loud.

"Really, Ethan? Is this a case of protesting just a bit too much? I saw the way you looked at her tonight."

"Looked at her? What do you mean?" he demanded, more than a little bit thrown by her questions.

"It's hard to describe. Half the time you looked as if you wanted to devour her. Seriously. You barely took your eyes off her all night and she was working equally as hard *not* to watch you. If I didn't know better, I'd say you two had met before or had some history together."

Ethan fought to keep his features composed. Sometimes his sister was too observant and she knew him too well.

"That's it, isn't it?" Tamsyn pressed. "You've met her before. When?"

"You're being ridiculous," he hedged. "If you're not prepared to cancel her contract then could you at least make sure you keep her out of my way as much as possible for the time she's here? For all our sakes." It wouldn't do much good if he couldn't keep her away from Tamsyn, too, but at least if Isobel wasn't around him, he might be able to think clearly and come up with a better plan.

He walked from Tamsyn's room, determined not to utter another word on the subject. But before he'd left, he'd seen the shrewdly assessing look in Tamsyn's eyes—and the light of mischief there. He groaned out loud when he got to his suite. He should have left well enough alone and not raised the subject with his sister. Now she'd be like a dog with a bone over it.

Two hours later he still couldn't sleep. Dressed only in pajama bottoms, he padded across the lushly carpeted floor to his windows and stared out in the darkness across to the cottage where Isobel was. As he stood there, a light flicked on inside the cottage. So, she couldn't sleep, either. He absently rubbed his belly, his hand stilling as he remembered her touch—her hand, her mouth, her tongue— at the very same spot last night.

Desire rolled through him and he closed his eyes briefly, seeing in his mind's eye the shimmer of her fair skin in the half light of the room, feeling its smooth softness beneath him. Feeling her.

His eyes flew open. The light at the cottage was still on. Damn. Ethan reached for the pull cord and yanked his drapes closed, but even knowing he'd blocked her from view, he couldn't help thinking that it looked like it was going to be a long night for them both.

Six

Isobel woke the next morning still furious. As if it wasn't enough that Ethan Masters had consumed her waking thoughts with his arrogance, his skillful lovemaking from the night before had infiltrated her sleep. As a result, she'd woken an aching, frustrated wreck, torn between the urge to track him down and slap him…or track him down and pounce on him. Not her best look, that was for sure, she decided as she surveyed herself in the bathroom mirror.

Thankfully, she didn't have to face anyone yet this morning. She'd asked for the time to herself, to familiarize herself with the property and the layout. To ease into the feel of the place so she could reflect its special character in the photos she was to create for their new marketing plan. She turned away from the mirror and started the shower running. During her usual jobs, showers were a rare luxury—and the one in this cabin was uncommonly nice. If only she could enjoy it without her head full of

distractions. A quick wash and rinse of her hair and she
was done and back out again.

Five minutes later, Isobel was dressed and busily sur-
veying the contents of the refrigerator in the very compact yet well-appointed kitchen. They really thought of
everything here, which gave her an idea. She grabbed one
of her cameras and took a few quick shots of the contents
of the fridge. Then, grabbing a banana, she went outside.

The land here was beautiful, especially in the early-
morning light. Row upon row of grapevines and frame-
work stretched across the land and up the hillside almost
as far as she could see. And there, up on the ridge of one
hill, stood a massive ruin. Her curiosity piqued, she pulled
the door of the cottage closed behind her and struck out
in that direction.

She'd raised a light sweat by the time she crested the
hill. Ahead of her rose the remains of what must have once
been a magnificent residence. Isobel spun in a slow circle. Clearly, from here, the house had overlooked the land
in all directions, almost like a castle set atop a mountain.
There was even a tower standing about four stories tall.

She walked closer, eyeing the red brick walls that
loomed above her, the gaping holes where windows were
once the eyes upon the valley below. A strange sadness
settled over her. So much destruction, so much loss. Here
and there plants had taken a hold in the brickwork, finding purchase in the most unlikely of places. Nature had a
way of doing that, she reminded herself. It reclaimed everything if left to do so.

She raised her camera, shooting off a series of shots,
fascinated by the play of light through the yawning window frames and the juxtaposition of new life and growth
with what had been the complete obliteration of a wealthy

home. The sound of hoofbeats and the creak of leather dragged her attention back to the here and now.

A large, dark horse cantered with incredible grace across the hard-packed ground, the man on its back no less beautiful. Her body recognized him before she could make out his face. Ethan reined in the horse a few meters in front of her.

"I didn't realize your charter included the ruin," he said stiffly, looking down the long blade of his nose at her.

"My *charter,* as you so eloquently put it, is to compile a collection of photos of the property, and specifically to create dossiers of pictures for each business center associated with The Masters. This is part of the property, is it not?"

She squinted up at him. Had he done that on purpose? Ridden toward her with the sun at his back to put her at a disadvantage?

"Part of its history, not its present." He swung one long denim-clad leg over the back of the horse and, letting go of the reins, kicked out of the other stirrup to drop, with the finesse of a large cat, to the ground. He took a few steps toward her.

"Aren't you worried he'll run away?" she asked, gesturing toward the horse.

Ethan shook his head. "He knows his place."

Isobel felt her lips pull into a smile. She had to hand it to the guy. He was nothing if not confident and completely self-assured. Her eyes raked over him, taking in the slightly mussed hair from his ride, the beat of his pulse at the open neck of his shirt, the way his cuffs were rolled up slightly exposing strong forearms. She rapidly averted her gaze before she did anything stupid, like start to send him the wrong signals.

Ethan Masters obviously knew his place, too. Master of all he surveyed. Looking out over the vineyard and the buildings below them, she had to admit that it was quite an estate that he lorded over. But that didn't mean she answered to him.

Ignoring every cell in her body, which demanded she stay within Ethan's orbit, she took a few steps away.

"I think I'll head back."

"So soon?"

There was a note to his voice that she didn't quite understand. Half snark, half enticement. He was a conundrum, all right. Last night he'd made it clear that she was persona non grata. At least as far as he was concerned. And yet, just now, he must have seen her here and had chosen to join her. He could easily have avoided talking to her.

Isobel shrugged. "I've been here awhile."

"Don't you want to hear the history behind Masters' Rise? Most do."

"I'm not most people, though, am I?"

He cocked his head slightly to one side, as if he was seeing her again but for the first time. "No, you're definitely not."

"It's not my habit to look at the past," she felt compelled to add. "I'm more about the here and now."

"An interesting trait," he commented.

"One I thought you might appreciate, given that you seem to want to forget we met before last night," she answered, the challenge clear in her voice.

"Touché," he said with a quirk of his lips. "Look, I'm sorry for how I reacted last night. It was uncalled for."

Isobel stared in surprise. An apology? From Ethan? Goodness—maybe the moon really was made of blue cheese after all.

"Apology accepted," she managed to say, biting her tongue to prevent herself from adding a smart-mouthed rejoinder.

Ethan gave a brief nod. "If you're heading back now, do you want a ride?"

"On that?" she asked.

There was little that frightened Isobel in this world, but horses were very near the top of that short list. In fact, she'd rather be sheltering under gunfire from tribal militia than climb on board that creature. No one said fear had to be rational.

"Afraid?"

There was a distinct challenge in that single word.

"Definitely," she said. "Thanks, but I'll walk."

"I won't let any harm come to you." He held out a hand. "Come on. Don't you trust me?"

She shook her head. "After last night, no. You made your feelings about me being here quite clear."

"Perhaps I'm merely being a good host."

Isobel snorted her disbelief. "Look, I said I'm happy to stay out of your way as much as I can, so how about you let me do that?"

Ethan fixed her with a hard stare, his chiseled lips set into a firm line of disapproval. Clearly, he was used to being obeyed, especially in his own domain. She held his gaze with her chin tilted up. Obedience had never been her strongest suit.

"Fine," he said after what felt like long minutes rather than seconds. "Tamsyn mentioned at breakfast that she plans to pick you up at the cottage at lunchtime for your full tour of the property today. Don't keep her waiting."

Ethan swung up onto the back of his horse and gathered the reins. Without another word he wheeled the beast around and headed back in the direction he'd arrived.

Isobel couldn't tear her eyes from the dashing figure he made on horseback. His long, powerful legs clamped to the horse's flanks, his body moving in synchronicity with the animal's gait. His fluidity and grace sent a wild spear of longing through her.

What would it have been like to double back with him? To feel the strength of his body supporting hers, to relinquish her safety to him and his ability to control the powerful animal beneath him? Isobel clenched her hands into tight fists and fought back the groan of frustration that built inside. Ethan had a powerful magnetism that pushed all her buttons every blasted time she came into contact with him. She needed to get a grip on herself or this contract would prove to be the most difficult and potentially dangerous one she'd ever embarked upon. Not physically, perhaps, but mentally—and she'd never, ever let anyone mess with her mind before.

She didn't plan to now, either.

Ethan checked the first of the ferments he had in progress and was relieved to have the distraction. What on earth had possessed him to talk to Isobel Fyfe this morning? He'd woken, determined to keep as much space between them as possible and had taken Obsidian for a much-needed dose of exercise and fresh air to clear his head. But the instant he'd seen a flash of color topped by the sun-kissed glow of blond hair, he'd headed toward the ruins. Even knowing it could only have been one person, he'd still gone there. Was he a closet masochist perhaps? he wondered scathingly as he considered his earlier actions.

She'd walked and climbed a fair distance and yet she'd looked as fresh and ready to tackle the return journey as she'd probably been when she'd started. She'd virtually glowed with health and vitality and he had to admire her fitness. He could attest personally to her physical strength, stamina and agility, and that memory hovered persistently at the back of his mind.

Relief warred with frustration at her refusal to ride back to the house with him. He wasn't used to being turned down, and for all he'd sworn he'd steer clear of her there was a part of him that still craved the warmth of her body hard against his—even if it was only on the back of a horse. He'd owed Isobel an apology; he'd given it. That was all.

Ethan shook his head and attempted to apply himself to his work. He had a meeting with Raif and Uncle Edward later today to discuss future planting programs and there was still plenty to attend to here at the winery. He was ever thankful that he had a strong team working with him. Without their hard work and support, especially through this fermentation period, he wouldn't be able to accomplish nearly as much. And he needed to accomplish something today—needed something to occupy his mind and energy so they wouldn't keep turning in the wrong direction.

He was particularly excited about the special reserve chardonnay they would soon be harvesting from The Masters reserve block. The oldest vines on the property, and the only ones to survive the fire that had decimated the house on the hill and virtually everything around it, they had been the backbone of the business as the family knew it today. There was a sense of pride and longevity in every vintage he'd been involved in and the harvest would be painstakingly handpicked before being crushed to extract the juice. The timing of the harvest was crucial to the outcome of the wine, as would be the fermentation process, but Ethan had full confidence in his team's ability to bring out the very best the crop had to offer.

He loved his work. Loved the science and the technicalities, as well as the romance and sensibilities involved in the making of the fine wines The Masters prided themselves on. And this part of the property, where the grapes reached their full potential, was his place.

A noise at the door made him stop what he was doing and turn to see who'd arrived.

"And this is the winery," Tamsyn said. "Where, according to Ethan, the magic begins, although I think Uncle Edward and Raif would have something to say about that because to them it's all about the vines."

Ethan's body went on high alert as Tamsyn and Isobel came toward him. Isobel had changed from her earlier attire and was wearing a soft floaty dress that alternately clung and flicked away around her legs. Legs he wasn't looking at, he reminded himself while dragging his eyes up her body.

"I'm showing Isobel around the property," Tamsyn said with a blithe smile, completely ignoring the daggers he was mentally throwing at her. "I thought we'd start here."

Before Ethan could respond, Tamsyn's cell phone began to trill and she excused herself to take the call.

"So this is where the magic begins, huh? With you?" Isobel said softly. "Who'd have thought?"

Ethan's eyes meshed with hers and he couldn't help thinking about the breathtaking magic they'd created together. Before he could answer, Tamsyn ended her call.

"Ethan, that was bridezilla's mom. I have to meet them at the restaurant to confirm the menus again. Looks like the apple didn't fall far from the tree with that bunch."

"Now?" he asked, struggling to keep a note of somewhat panicked displeasure from his tone.

"Sure, now. Nothing with that family is ever anything less than immediate. You can look after Isobel, right?" She turned to Isobel and gave her a quick hug. "Sorry to dump you on my brother, but if I don't get back here in the next couple of hours, I'll still see you for a drink before dinner, okay?"

And then she was gone. Leaving him alone, quite deliberately he suspected, with the one woman he would have preferred on the other side of the world.

"Look, I'll just take care of myself," Isobel began. "It's obvious you're busy."

Every cell in his body urged him to accept her offer but a perverse alter ego pushed him to reply in the negative. Did she think he couldn't control himself around her, couldn't be the flawless host and tour guide the situation required him to be? She would learn that there was little he could not do, once he set his mind to it.

"I can spare a few minutes to show you around."

"Look, only if you're sure it's no bother."

"Come on," he said, gesturing for her to follow.

"Why do I get the impression you've neglected to say 'Let's get this over with' at the end of that?"

There was a barely suppressed bubble of laughter at the back of her voice and he felt his lips tug reluctantly into a wry smile in response. "I didn't say that." Though apparently, it was completely obvious that that was what he'd been thinking.

She laughed out loud at his dry response. "Look, why don't we start as if we have never met before."

Ethan looked at her askance. "You have to be kidding, right?"

Even now her light scent filled his nostrils. He could still vividly remember the feel of her body against his, the taste of her skin, the sensation of joining with her in the most intimate of possible ways. No, there was no way on this earth that he was capable of pretending they'd never met before, never shared the closeness and familiarity with one another's bodies that they'd experienced.

"Yeah, okay, you're right. It was worth a shot." She looked around the area they were in, taking in the large tanks and barrels that lined the walls. "This really is where it happens, isn't it? Can you walk me through what has to take place to get to this point and what it is that you do here?"

"I thought you were a photographer, not a wannabe winemaker."

Isobel shrugged. "I like to understand my subjects before I begin to work. Makes it easier to know what is important and what isn't."

Ethan gave her an assessing look, taken aback by how genuinely interested she appeared. He launched into a description of the coordination of tasks that were required between the vineyard and the winery and was challenged by the astute questions she asked in a bid for more information. By the time he was leading her through the building to the main entrance, a couple of hours had flown by.

She was surprisingly good company, though all along his body had been buoyed by a buzz of latent attraction that simmered beneath the surface. He'd tried to avoid physical contact, but on those few occasions their hands had brushed as they walked along, he'd been shocked by the flare of hunger and desire that had flashed through him.

Their attraction was dangerously addictive, her proximity here at The Masters all too enticingly near. He had to create some distance or the next few weeks would be absolute hell.

He was surprised to see Tamsyn walking toward the winery as he and Isobel left the building.

"Meeting go okay?" he asked as his sister drew nearer.

"Well, we have a consensus—for today, at least," Tamsyn said with a weary smile.

His sister looked from him to Isobel and back again. He could see the light of an unasked question clear in her eyes and it forced him into making a decision.

"Now that you're back to take care of Ms. Fyfe, I'm off to see Shanal."

"Shanal? Today?"

He didn't answer Tamsyn directly but turned instead to Isobel. "Let me know if you need more information and when you plan to start shooting."

"Sure, thanks for your time."

She sounded polite, professional and as far removed from the lover whose skin he'd explored thoroughly with both his hands and his mouth as it was possible to be. And yet, despite all that, he still felt that zing of awareness when she held out her hand to shake his. The instant his hand enveloped hers he wanted to tug her toward him, wrap her in his arms and kiss her like he'd been aching to do since last night.

As if her hand was suddenly and unbearably hot, he let her go, gave Tamsyn a nod and turned back to the winery. As delectable as Isobel Fyfe's company had been, he wasn't going to go there again. He'd have to be wary around her, especially given her growing friendship with Tamsyn. Could he trust her with what she knew? Could he be certain that she wouldn't take it upon herself to share with his sister the information he wanted to keep only to himself?

Only time would tell, he thought as he lifted his phone to his ear, the auto dial already punching through to Shanal Peat's mobile. There was no way he could know for sure, unless he was prepared to spend day in and day out at Isobel's side—and right now, as disconcerting as the thought had been, and as emphatic as he'd been about keeping some distance between them, it also held tantalizing appeal.

Seven

Isobel looked around the gathering. Friday night looked to be friends' night at The Masters, and the swell of people stretched across the back lawn and wide veranda of the main house looked as if they were well used to the company and the surroundings. One arrival had interested her the most. The woman was an exotic beauty with mixed Indian and Australian heritage that made Isobel's fingers itch to reach for her camera and capture the play of late-afternoon light across Shanal Peat's exquisite features.

She looked around for Ethan, expecting to see him here already.

"Looking for my brother?" Tamsyn asked from beside her.

"No, not really," Isobel protested but even she knew the conviction in her voice was weak.

"He's still at the winery, although I'm sure when he hears that Shanal is here, he'll be over. This is usually his most antisocial time of the year so I'm surprised he invited her today." Tamsyn gave Isobel an assessing look even as she hung on the arm of a tall, leanly built man with sandy hair and blue eyes. "Unless he thinks he needs the added protection, that is."

"Not from me, that's for certain," Isobel said firmly.

All week Tamsyn had been passing remarks about her brother and Isobel that had been laden with innuendo, and all week Isobel had been deflecting them as carefully as she could. It didn't help that every time she'd caught a glimpse of the man in question she'd felt her heart rate speed up while a flush of heat, and something more, spread through her body. Each member of the Masters family was charming and attractive, certainly more so than any one family deserved or ought to be, but Ethan seemed to be the only one who hit her hot button.

"Have you met my fiancé yet?" Tamsyn asked. "Trent works for a law firm in the city—too hard, I might add. Trent, this is Isobel Fyfe. She's the photographer I was telling you about. Isobel, Trent Mayweather."

"Pleased to meet you," Isobel said, extending her hand.

She was surprised when Trent only gripped the tip of her fingers and gave her a halfhearted shake. The action rankled with her and made her feel as if she was being treated as undeserving of the full force of his attention. Swiftly, she pushed her negative thoughts aside. The guy was probably only being polite and didn't want to inflict a bone crusher on her. Besides, he was Tamsyn's fiancé and the other woman was very clearly in love with the man at her side. There must be more to him than she was seeing at the moment. Maybe she'd just caught him at the tail end of a bad day.

"And you," he said in a voice as smooth as his *GQ* attire

and expertly styled hair. "I followed your blog while you were in Africa last month. It's great work you do there."

The guy jumped in her estimation.

"Thanks. I do what I can to raise public awareness. I'm planning to head back after this assignment."

"But weren't you—"

"Invited to leave?" Isobel said with a broad smile. "Yes, but I have my methods. I'm confident I can get back and finish what I'd set out to do."

Trent nodded. "I admire your tenacity. I don't think I'd be as brave."

"Actually, bravery doesn't really enter into it," she replied. "I'm sure you have situations in your work where you're not prepared to back down, no matter the incentive to do so."

"You're right," he conceded. "Although the danger levels are perhaps a little less obvious in the Supreme Court."

Isobel laughed at his dry observation but the mirth dried in her throat as she caught sight of Ethan arriving and making a beeline directly for the beautiful Shanal Peat. As she watched, the other woman's sea-green eyes lit up at the new arrival and her mobile lips curved into a smile of welcome. Isobel couldn't ignore the stab of envy that pierced her as Ethan smiled with genuine warmth at Shanal and bent to kiss those lips. She turned her back on the happy reunion and focused anew on something Trent was saying. The last thing she wanted to do was be a voyeur…the second to last thing she wanted was to admit to herself why it bothered her so much to see Ethan up close and personal with another woman.

She'd seen very little of him this week. She'd heard he'd been busy with the ferments and coordinating the cellar work, plus a Shiraz harvest from a vineyard outside the home estate, and he hadn't even made it to dinner each evening. In fact, she'd heard more than enough about his day-to-day activities from Tamsyn whenever the opportunity arose. Now, finally in the same room with him again, every cell in her body urged her to turn around, to drink in the sight of him, to try and quell the yearning desire that simmered in her body and colored every moment of every day she was here.

Sure, he was overbearing and a bit on the authoritative side. In most guys that was just too much. But in Ethan, especially here, in his home patch, it was simply who he was—like it or not. Each family member had their own area of expertise, was in charge of their own minibusiness within the whole that was The Masters, yet all deferred to Ethan in their own way. Clearly, with the death of his father, he'd become the head of the family and now, having seen the family, she realized what a massive responsibility lay on his broad shoulders. It explained a lot about his attitude. Growing up he must have always known he'd be in charge one day. He was the type to relish that responsibility rather than shirk or shy away from it. And from the looks of things, he'd taken his duty to protect the family very seriously—especially when it came to protecting his sister from the risk of getting hurt.

Tamsyn and Trent made their excuses to Isobel and drifted away to welcome another newcomer, and Isobel gave in to her need to turn around. For a moment she felt as if she was adrift as Ethan was not in her immediate line of sight. But then she caught the sound of his voice, his laughter, and tracked him down.

Her insides melted at the sound of his laugh. It was rich and full and unabashed in its joy. Again, that pang of envy speared her as she realized that it was Shanal who was the cause of his mirth. It seemed she was the only one here who was capable of lightening his dark countenance and showing another side to this multifaceted man.

It was a good thing she was only here for another few weeks, Isobel thought with a small shiver that was in direct contrast to the warmth thrown out by several gas heaters positioned around the property. Any more of this torment and she'd be a blithering wreck by the time she left. She didn't belong here, with this well-established family and their well-established life. Nothing drove that point home like seeing the kind of woman that Ethan Masters so clearly wanted by his side. Everything about her, from her polished appearance to her quiet, flawless manners, to her easy and clearly well-established familiarity with Ethan's family members was in direct contrast with Isobel.

It was rare that Isobel found herself wanting. She'd never lacked for confidence before, but somehow, in this crowd, she realized that despite all her protestations to the contrary, some things had definitely been missing from her life, and this full sense of family and belonging were among them.

Ethan looked up from his conversation with Shanal and found Isobel looking directly at them. Looking, but not seeing. Her eyes were unfocused, her expression empty of her usual vivacity. Briefly, he wondered what was wrong, before something Shanal said dragged his attention back again. But it wasn't long before his eyes lifted again, searching the gathering for Isobel's cap of light blond hair.

He saw her over by the table on the veranda that was now groaning with food. She had a plate but even from this distance he could see she barely had anything on it. His protective instincts rose to the fore.

"Um, Ethan? Are you still listening to me?" Shanal asked with a smile on her face.

He looked at her, struck anew by the perfect symmetry of her face and her exotic coloring. She had to be the most beautiful woman he knew, and probably the most intelligent at the same time. And yet... His gaze flicked to Isobel before he forced himself to respond to his guest.

"I'm sorry. It's been a busy few days," he said with an apologetic smile.

"And going to get busier, too, I imagine," she replied, laying a hand on his arm to show she accepted his apology. "Which reminds me, I can't stay too late tonight. I need to check on some data I'm collating on the new strain of organic seed stock."

"We'd better hit the buffet then. We can't let you go home hungry."

They walked arm in arm to the veranda and Ethan was struck by how comfortable he felt with Shanal. After all, they'd known each other since their first week at university, had even shared an apartment together for a while. The ease he felt in her company made him sure about his decision to court her and hopefully, eventually, marry her. Although that ease also made him wonder about the lack of chemistry between them. They were a pair of healthy adults in the prime of their lives. Shouldn't there be something there?

He mentally shrugged the question away. There'd be time enough for that in the future. For now he was content to know that being with Shanal didn't leave him constantly on edge, or worse, constantly in a state of arousal that shattered his legendary concentration and focus and made him crave things that had no place in his life. Things? No, not things—a person. More specifically, Isobel Fyfe.

She was at the end of the veranda, a pashmina slung with casual elegance around her shoulders, while she talked to Zac Peters, Tamsyn's assistant and the brainchild for the marketing side of The Masters. Isobel listened intently to something Zac said, and he wondered what it was that held her attention so keenly. It was probably the most still he'd ever seen her and the fall of her straight hair almost completely shielded her face, hiding its mobile expressiveness and adding to the impression of stillness. As he looked, he remembered how that hair was soft and silky and felt like a million dollars as it stroked over his skin. He uttered an involuntary groan.

"You okay?" Shanal asked, her brow creased with concern.

"I'm fine," he hastened to assure her, but he was anything but.

Just like that, Isobel had woven her way past his defenses again. The woman was addictive and it seemed the harder he tried to resist her allure, the more he was drawn to her. Maybe that was it. Maybe he just needed to get her out of his system. He'd always sneered when he'd heard people tell of that before, but now he had an inkling as to how they felt. The compulsion to follow through on his thoughts was like a match to dry straw.

He shepherded Shanal to the opposite end of the veranda, where Isobel wouldn't be in his line of sight and gave his attention to the woman he, in all honesty, was most relaxed with. They were friends, good friends, and it was time to see if they could move their friendship up to the next level. It was about an hour later that Shanal looked at her watch.

"I'd better be on my way. Thank you so much for including me this evening. It's been lovely. I always enjoy your company."

"As I do yours," Ethan said, injecting his voice with more feeling than usual. He laid a hand at the small of Shanal's back. "Here, let me see you to your car."

They walked around the side of the house to the main driveway, which was lined with visitors' cars. He stopped by Shanal's practical silver compact. Imported, stylish and elegant, the car was like her in many ways. Chic but not fussy. Attractive but not over the top. She unlocked the doors with a press of her remote and Ethan reached to open her door for her. Before she could get in, however, he gathered her closer and leaned down to kiss her. The press of their lips was fleeting, pleasant but certainly not ground shaking, and it was over almost before it had begun with Shanal being the first to pull away.

"Thanks again for tonight," she said, ducking her head as she got into the car. "I had a really lovely time."

"Me, too," Ethan said. "How about dinner later next week?"

"Sure. I'm not certain how my diary is looking but give me a call, okay?"

And then she was gone. As he watched her car wind along the driveway and toward the main road he wondered if he was indeed doing the right thing by deciding to shift the course of their friendship. He mulled the question over as he walked back to the gathering. Isobel was the first person he saw as he rounded the side of the house and that zing of awareness poured through his veins.

How was it that he could feel more for a woman like Isobel Fyfe than for Shanal, who he'd known for almost half of his life? For the rest of the get-together the answer eluded him. Still, it kept tickling at the back of his mind as he went through the motions of circulating through the guests he hadn't spoken with yet and spending a little time with each family member to catch up on their days.

It was nearing midnight when the last of the guests had finally driven off. He knew he should go up to bed, tomorrow was going to be another demanding day. Instead, he found his feet were tracking quietly along the path toward Isobel's cottage. He hadn't seen her leave, but he'd heard from Tamsyn that she'd helped with clearing things away to the kitchen before slipping off after saying good-night. Had she been avoiding him? Probably, and with good reason if she'd been suffering the same form of physical discomfort as he had these past few days. Or maybe she was taking him at his word. Staying away from him exactly as he'd asked. Asked? Who was he kidding?

It was sheer madness going to see her now, but it was something he knew he had to do. Perhaps if he confronted the pull drawing him to her, he could lay the demons of his attraction to her to rest once and for all. A voice inside him laughed. Who was he kidding? He wanted her like he'd wanted no other woman ever before. Desire drummed in his blood, a constant reminder of what they'd once shared. What he wanted to share with her again. Anonymous, meaningless release. But could it be that still? She was no longer the complete stranger she'd been the evening they'd met.

Before he knew it he was at the entrance to her cottage, his hand poised and ready to knock. He could leave now. She'd never know he was here. If he did, there'd be no recriminations come morning. No regrets.

He knocked at the door.

Eight

Ethan filled the doorway, framed in the soft light that bathed the front entrance.

"Ethan? What—?"

Isobel never got to finish her question. Her answer, such as it was, was immediate in the envelopment of his arms, and the searing, questing fierceness of his kiss. Her arms instinctively reached up, her hands linking at the back of his neck and holding him to her. Her feet arching onto tiptoes so she could meet him on a more level ground. Her body aligning with his, softness against muscle. And it felt so good.

She hadn't realized until right this moment just how much she'd craved him. Wanted his strength, desired his touch, needed his possession.

Dimly, Isobel was aware of being buoyed backward, of the solid thud of the wooden door closing behind Ethan's back, but then her senses filled once more with him—

gloriously, excitedly overflowing with anticipation and eagerness.

Their lips were still joined, their tongues engaged in a sensual dance of remembrance.

He dragged his mouth away, resting his forehead against her own, his breathing ragged and raw.

"Tell me you don't want this and I'll go."

She bracketed his face with her hands and looked deep into his dark brown eyes, eyes that glowed with passion and need.

"I want you," she said softly.

"Thank you." He sighed.

Isobel couldn't help but smile a small private smile. Even in this he couldn't help but be straitlaced and proper. But she knew there were two distinct sides to Ethan Masters. There was the leader and family chieftain, and then there was the lover—it was the lover who'd come to her tonight. The lover who would stoke her internal fires until she was raging with heat, until she'd explode like a supernova burning bright in a distant sky.

Ethan's hands shoved at the waist of her pajama bottoms, making the cotton drawstring pants drop to her feet. His palms cupped her buttocks, pulling her firmly against him, against the hardness that showed her more than words could ever say, what effect she had on him.

She felt her body quicken instantly and she pulled his shirt free of his trousers and yanked his buttons open, heedless to the damage she wrought in her quest to feel his skin beneath her hands, her lips, her tongue.

He smelled divine, and she inhaled deeply, drawing in the scent of his skin and storing it away in her memory because she knew this—his presence, his overwhelming need for her—was an irregularity in his world. She'd take what she could get and she would cherish it to carry with her when she left again.

Ethan's hands moved slowly up her body, dragging the tank top she'd paired with her pajama pants up over her body as he went, exposing her to his hungry gaze. Her nipples grew tight and her breasts felt full and aching—wanting his touch above all else. His fingers softly skimmed their roundness, barely touching her yet igniting a line of fire that shot straight to her core, making her inner muscles clench on a wave of sensation.

She pushed at his shirt with her hands, dragging it off him and dropping it to the floor, then pressed herself into the hard plane of his chest. The ache, rather than being relieved, intensified into a raw demand that had dwelt just below the surface this entire past week. Patience, never her strongest point, deserted her completely. She grabbed for his belt, tugging it loose and unfastening his trousers with surprising finesse. She shoved at his pants and slipped her hand inside the waistband of his boxer briefs, pulling the fabric away and letting the hard length of his desire spring against her palm. Her fingers closed around him and she felt him shudder. She loved the feel of him, the texture of his skin, the engorged strength and leashed power, the silken head. She stroked his length and felt him shudder again.

His fingers closed around hers.

"Not yet, I'm too close, too desperate for you to touch me like that right now," he said in a strained voice.

"I like desperate," she whispered in response and clenched him that little bit tighter.

He drew in a sharp breath. "Soon," he said roughly. "Very soon."

Ethan guided her hand away from him and caught her mouth in a kiss that claimed her totally. His hands skimmed up the length of her back, sending thrills of delight running through her. His thigh pressed between her legs, affording a brief respite to the longing that gathered at the apex of her thighs, but she knew it wouldn't be enough for long.

She ground against him, seeking more pressure, seeking release. The muscles of his thigh beneath her were so firm, the hairs on his leg abrading the insides of her legs in a tantalizing contrast to the smoothness of her own.

"Okay, you win," Ethan groaned, pulling away from her and spinning her around. "Hold on to the back of the sofa," he instructed roughly.

She felt him shift behind her and bend to retrieve something from his trouser pocket. And then she felt the warm, blunt probe of his erection between her legs. She arched her back downward, raising her hips and spreading her legs that little more. His hands, warm and smooth and strong, were at her hips. She pushed back and felt his tip ease inside her.

It felt so good, but it wasn't enough. She needed him all—all the way. Finally, he thrust against her, stretching and filling her so deeply it all but took her breath away. And then he began to move, and the pressure inside her built higher. She wanted to draw out each acute delight but her body, and his, had other ideas. Her climax rushed upon her, making her legs shake and her inner muscles spasm in tight coils of ecstasy over and over, forcing her to cry out loud, lost in the web of sensation that caught her in its thrall.

She felt Ethan stiffen, his hips pressed hard against her, his body jerking as his own climax took him. His fingers were still tight on her hips—she'd probably have marks there tomorrow but she didn't care. How could she when they were so good together, so incendiary?

His grip softened, his palms once more skimming her heated flesh, stroking her, soothing her. He lowered himself over her back and pressed a kiss against her nape, which sent a corresponding shiver the length of her spine and made her insides tighten once more.

"I can't stay away from you," he said softly against her shoulder. "I've tried and I just can't do it."

Her heart contracted in response to the helplessness in his voice. She felt the same way but she knew it was a fleeting thing they shared. Isobel understood fleeting. She also knew that when something was short-lived it paid to grab it with both hands to make the most of it, and worry about the consequences later.

"Then don't try," she answered, her voice shaking with the aftermath of what they'd just shared.

"But why you? Why now?" he asked.

"Does it matter?" She sighed softly. "Let's just be together, for now."

"I can do that," he answered, kissing her nape again as he carefully withdrew from her body.

She straightened and forced herself to turn around, almost afraid to see what might be in his eyes when she met them.

"Come on," she said, holding out her hand. "Come to bed with me."

He stood still as a statue, and equally as beautiful, before taking her hand in silent acquiescence. They left their clothing where it lay, scattered on the sitting room floor, and walked together to her bedroom. The king-size bed was already rumpled, evidence of how much she'd already tossed and turned in the short time she'd been in bed before Ethan's knock had propelled her to the door. Isobel pulled back the sheets and climbed onto the bed, pulling Ethan after her.

She understood how much it had cost him to come to her tonight. He'd been aloof toward her all week, and she could see why. She could understand the level of responsibility he bore on his shoulders and why it was so important to him to live up to his family's expectations. A life like the Masters family enjoyed was so far from what she was used to, but it didn't mean she had no empathy for Ethan as the new head of what was arguably a dynasty.

For a man with his pride, to crumble and come to her door as he had tonight, he had to be at war within himself. And she knew all about the ravages of war. How it displaced families, how it destroyed livelihoods and both past and present. War, whether physical or mental, always exacted a price. The question was would this be at his cost, or hers?

Isobel pushed Ethan down against the bed, her hands gently roaming the curves and valleys of his body, coaxing a response from him that wasn't driven from a place of anger or fear...or of loathing. Because that was what she was frightened of. That he might loathe her or at least loathe what this attraction between them was doing to him. That it was making him lose precious control.

This was all about giving that control back to him. Because the more comfortable he felt with the draw that existed between them, the more likely it was that he'd indulge himself in exploring it for as long as she stayed at The Masters.

She peppered a line of kisses along his collarbone then down the center of his chest. His arms came up around her, his hands drifting up and down the line of her spine. Isobel felt her body respond in degrees. The shimmering heat of desire kept building and building within her as she stoked the same heat within him. By the time she reached for the side pocket of her pack, which she kept beside the bed, she was more than ready to feel the heavy weight of his body within hers.

Ethan barely said a word, watching her with eyes that glittered like chips of dark volcanic glass, as she extracted a condom and slowly, carefully, smoothed it over the straining length of his flesh. She positioned herself above him and held him in one hand, guiding him to the secret part of her body that ached for his possession. He rose up as she sank onto him, her body stretching to accommodate him, her eyes fluttered closed as a sigh of gratification eased from her at the rightness of this union between their bodies.

His hands gripped her hips, holding her steady when she wanted to rock against him. Her eyes flicked open, locking with his. Only then did he loosen his hold on her and allow her to move. She moaned at that first movement, at the sensations that spread out through her body, at the intensity of the connection between them as they continued to look directly into one another's eyes. Time blurred as she rocked against him, her movements deliberate and slow, until she could barely take it any longer. Beads of perspiration dotted her face, her body, matching the sheen across his as they remained locked together in a sensual wave of motion. A wave that built and built, taking her closer and closer to the edge.

Ethan suddenly shifted, holding her hips and maintaining their union even as he slid her beneath him and settled between her legs. He kept up their momentum, driving her to even greater heights before slowing down again. Just when she thought she was incapable of feeling any more, he upped the tempo. In seconds she was spiraling high, higher than she'd ever been as wave after building wave of pleasure resonated through her body. As her body clenched around him, she felt Ethan stiffen before he plunged into her, again and again until a shout clawed its way from deep in his throat and he shuddered against her.

He rolled to the side, taking her with him, his breathing ragged, his eyes now closed, his pulse beating like a crazy thing at the base of his throat. She leaned forward and kissed him, right there, at that exact spot that evidenced the passion they'd just shared. His skin was hot, slick and slightly salty. She stroked her hand across his chest in a lazy sweep, not wanting for a second to lose that link they'd so tenuously established.

Ethan's eyes opened, and one of his hands closed around hers, holding it firmly against his chest.

"Thank you," he said, his voice a low rumble.

"Thank you?"

"For not telling me to get the hell out of here."

She smiled. "What, and miss all this?" She squeezed her internal muscles, teasing him in voice and deed.

Some of the tension that had begun to appear on his face eased away.

He shook his head slightly. "Don't you take anything seriously?"

"I take my work seriously," she replied. "But everything else, well, that's fluid."

"What's that like?" he asked, releasing her hand and reaching out to twist a length of her hair around his finger.

"It's freedom. Unless it impacts directly on my work, I don't have to worry about what other people think, or say, or do. I look after myself and I like it that way."

"No plans to ever settle down in one place?"

She shook her head emphatically. "Definitely not. I've moved around for most of my life. I couldn't imagine doing it differently, or why I'd want to."

He relaxed a little more and she wondered for a second if he'd been worried that now they'd made love again that she might begin to put demands upon him, expect more than just the amazing sex they shared.

A fleeting pang of regret pierced her chest but she pushed it aside. She didn't do long term. She just didn't. This, whatever they had, was just fine by her. For however long they had it. Now that Ethan had climbed down off his high horse, maybe they could just enjoy each other for the time she was here.

"Is that why you chose photography as your career?" he asked, continuing to twirl her hair between his fingers.

"It's certainly flexible, but that isn't why I do it. It chose me, I suppose. When my dad and I left New Zealand, and started traveling, one of his friends gave me an old SLR camera. I played around with it—discovered I had a knack for composition. It wasn't long before I became fascinated with the play of light and darkness on life."

"That sounds deep," Ethan commented with a smile.

"I don't spend all my life doing catalog work, you know." She laughed lightly.

"So what do you do the rest of the time?"

The laughter fled from inside her as she recalled her last photo assignment in Africa. Recalled the heat, the smells, the poverty. The destitution and helplessness of the people being rousted out of their homes and livings by a despotic and avaricious leader. And how, even in that desolation, there was still hope. Hope for something better, for someone or some nation to help. That was Isobel's mission. To show the world the people who needed help. To bring that desperation into more privileged peoples' and their governments' consciousness. To help, somehow, and give those struggling people some hope.

"I take photos of people. Families, mostly."

She worked hard to keep her voice light. There was a time and a place for discussing what she did and that wasn't here or right now. It was why she kept a very successful blog running on her visits to areas like the one she'd just been expelled from and why, when she was away from those areas, she lived her life to the fullest, with color, with joy.

"What, like mall photographers? Grumpy babies and toddlers?"

"Not quite," Isobel amended, weighing up whether or not to go deeper into what she did with Ethan.

The decision was taken from her hands when he let her hair go and rose from the bed.

"I'll get rid of this and then get going," he said, referring to the used condom.

"You don't want to stay?"

She wasn't upset that he planned to leave her now that his passion for her had been sated. Or at least that's what she told herself.

"I have an early start tomorrow. I don't want to disturb you. Besides, I don't think it's a good idea if we make a habit of this."

His emotional shutters were back down. She could see it as plain as day on his face, and for some stupid reason it hurt her deep inside. What had she been hoping for? A declaration of his feelings for her? A promise to make every night as spectacular as this one had been? She gave herself a mental shake. That wasn't what she wanted.

Liar, a voice in the back of her mind whispered piercingly through her consciousness.

She shoved the thought back just as swiftly as it came. As he headed to the bathroom to clean up, she rolled out of bed and walked naked into the living room to pick up Ethan's clothes, as well as drag her pajamas back over her body.

He came out of the bathroom and uttered his thanks as

she silently handed him his things. He gave her a brief, chaste kiss once he was dressed, and then he was gone. Isobel turned off the lights behind her as she went back to bed and curled into a ball where he'd lain. Telling herself she was all sorts of pathetic for wishing him back here at her side even as she tried not to inhale the faint traces of his scent on the pillow where his head had lain only minutes before.

It seemed that from the moment she'd met Ethan Masters her life had been thrown into a state of heightened awareness and confusion. Despite his being the antithesis to the way she lived her life, she remained inexorably drawn to him. *It's just the sex,* she told herself. And yes, it was great sex. Off-the-scale sex. Better than she'd ever had in her entire life sex. But they were two very different people.

She was transient, lived her life out of a backpack and traveled wherever whim took her. He was established, had generations of history behind him and backing him from sunup to sundown. He was grounded in the earth here as much as those vineyards she'd walked through several times this past week. Perhaps even more so.

He was a commitment kind of guy. A guy who looked great with a woman like Shanal Peat on his arm and in his life. Try as she might, Isobel couldn't quell the fierce sense of possessiveness that swept through her. She didn't want to think about Ethan with Shanal, or with any woman, for that matter. But, she reminded herself firmly, she was only here for, at most, three more weeks—whereas Ethan would be here for the rest of his life.

Forever—it wasn't the kind of thing she could commit to, nor wanted to, she told herself as she rolled to her other side. She dragged the bedcovers over her now-chilled body and told herself that the bed didn't feel half-empty without Ethan lying by her side.

Nine

Whatever he'd been thinking by going to Isobel on Friday night, it had been the wrong thing to do, Ethan decided as he roamed the winery late on Sunday.

Everyone had gone to bed, leaving him alone with his thoughts and his work. This was his favorite stage of production, and he took his work very seriously—checking and rechecking everything. Overseeing whatever he'd delegated so thoroughly, he may as well have done it all himself. Tam teased him about being a control freak but he felt no shame in wanting to ensure that The Masters label maintained its hard-won profile in the marketplace.

Yet tonight was different. He struggled to concentrate on his tasks, his mind constantly sliding back in time to Friday. To the expression on Isobel's face when she'd opened her door to him. To her easy acceptance of what he'd been there for. To the feel of her limbs wrapped tight around his.

Ethan pushed a trembling hand through his hair and tried to shake the images of Isobel's long back, her tapered waist, and her rounded buttocks from his mind. She hadn't hesitated when he'd turned her around, hadn't balked when he'd driven into her body like a crazy man. She'd accepted everything, and then taken him to her bed where she'd given to him all over again.

Then, when he'd so abruptly left her, she hadn't so much as batted an eyelid. Not a single plea to him to remain had passed her lips, although he knew he'd have been welcome.

In fact, the lure of her warm and accepting body had been strong. Too strong. He'd known it would have been all too easy to stay in her bed, in her arms, all night long. He already felt too vulnerable—too exposed in his endless desire for her. Sleeping beside her would only let her further behind his defenses. She read him far too well as it was. And she'd already proven she could manipulate him with ease.

Oh, sure, their pleasure had been mutual, but in hindsight, Ethan could see that she'd been the one in charge all along, no matter what he'd thought at the time. The realization was an eye opener. He was used to taking charge, to being the boss, and she'd turned the tables on him without him even noticing.

And here she was, still stuck firmly in his mind. He'd even had lunch today with Shanal. That had been far less promising than he'd hoped. They'd walked the botanical gardens at Mt. Lofty before heading out to a nearby café, and despite his best efforts, there'd been no zing when he'd taken her hand, no excitement when he'd embraced her after returning her to her home. He knew she'd felt the same way. She'd presented her cheek for a kiss to avoid kissing him on the lips.

It left him feeling out of sorts. Not irritated, exactly,

but something close to that. He just couldn't understand it. He and Shanal were perfect for each other. Always had been. And they knew each other so well—were comfortable together. So why was there no spark?

And, more important, why had he spent half the time with Shanal wondering what Isobel was up to today? He'd seen her drive off with Cade earlier on and had felt a surge of jealousy so strong it had left a very nasty taste in his mouth. He didn't do jealousy and he had no right to, either. After all, hadn't *he* been out with Shanal at the very same time?

He and Isobel had slept together. Twice. That was all. He had no claim over her. If she wanted to she could sleep with all the men in his family and he had no rights to stop her.

His head began to pound and an irrational sense of possessiveness clawed at his gut. He shook his head. This was ridiculous. Even here, in his sanctuary—the winery, the one place where he could always find solace in his work— she still invaded his thoughts.

The sound of a car driving slowly along the drive toward the main house caught his attention. He looked outside his window and saw Cade's car turn up the small driveway that led to Isobel's cottage. It seemed to Ethan that it lingered there an inordinately long time before swinging around and heading back to the main house.

Ethan tried desperately to ignore the not so subtle urging in the back of his mind. The one that told him to go to Isobel. To find out for himself what she'd been up to with his cousin all day. Before he was even aware of it he was turning off the lights at the winery and locking the door behind him, his feet treading the pathway to her cottage as they had only two nights ago.

Through the cottage window he could see her seated at the dining table, her laptop in front of her and a slideshow

OFFICIAL OPINION POLL

Dear Reader,

Since you are a book enthusiast, we would like to know what you think.

Inside you will find a short Opinion Poll. Please participate in our poll by sharing your opinion on 3 subjects that are very important to all of us.

To thank you for your participation, we would like to send you **2 FREE BOOKS** and **2 FREE GIFTS!**

Please enjoy them with our compliments.

Sincerely,

Pam Powers

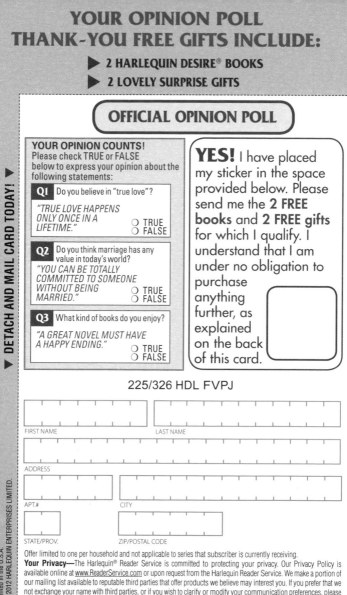

YOUR OPINION POLL
THANK-YOU FREE GIFTS INCLUDE:

▶ **2 HARLEQUIN DESIRE® BOOKS**
▶ **2 LOVELY SURPRISE GIFTS**

◀ **DETACH AND MAIL CARD TODAY!** ▶

OFFICIAL OPINION POLL

YOUR OPINION COUNTS!
Please check TRUE or FALSE below to express your opinion about the following statements:

Q1 Do you believe in "true love"?

"TRUE LOVE HAPPENS ONLY ONCE IN A LIFETIME."
○ TRUE
○ FALSE

Q2 Do you think marriage has any value in today's world?

"YOU CAN BE TOTALLY COMMITTED TO SOMEONE WITHOUT BEING MARRIED."
○ TRUE
○ FALSE

Q3 What kind of books do you enjoy?

"A GREAT NOVEL MUST HAVE A HAPPY ENDING."
○ TRUE
○ FALSE

YES! I have placed my sticker in the space provided below. Please send me the **2 FREE books** and **2 FREE gifts** for which I qualify. I understand that I am under no obligation to purchase anything further, as explained on the back of this card.

225/326 HDL FVPJ

FIRST NAME

LAST NAME

ADDRESS

APT.#

CITY

STATE/PROV.

ZIP/POSTAL CODE

Offer limited to one per household and not applicable to series that subscriber is currently receiving.

Your Privacy—The Harlequin® Reader Service is committed to protecting your privacy. Our Privacy Policy is available online at www.ReaderService.com or upon request from the Harlequin Reader Service. We make a portion of our mailing list available to reputable third parties that offer products we believe may interest you. If you prefer that we not exchange your name with third parties, or if you wish to clarify or modify your communication preferences, please visit us at www.ReaderService.com/consumerchoice or write to us at Harlequin Reader Service Preference Service, P.O. Box 9062, Buffalo, NY 14269. Include your complete name and address.

Accepting your 2 free books and 2 free gifts (gifts valued at approximately $10.00) places you under no obligation to buy anything. You may keep the books and gifts and return the shipping statement marked "cancel." If you do not cancel, about a month later we'll send you 6 additional books and bill you just $4.30 each in the U.S. or $4.99 each in Canada. That is a savings of at least 14% off the cover price. It's quite a bargain! Shipping and handling is just 50¢ per book in the U.S. and 75¢ per book in Canada.* You may cancel at any time, but if you choose to continue, every month we'll send you 6 more books, which you may either purchase at the discount price or return to us and cancel your subscription.

*Terms and prices subject to change without notice. Prices do not include applicable taxes. Sales tax applicable in N.Y. Canadian residents will be charged applicable taxes. Offer not valid in Quebec. Books received may not be as shown. All orders subject to credit approval. Credit or debit balances in a customer's account(s) may be offset by any other outstanding balance owed by or to the customer. Please allow 4 to 6 weeks for delivery. Offer available while quantities last.

If offer card is missing write to: Harlequin Reader Service, P.O. Box 1867, Buffalo NY 14240-1867 or visit: www.ReaderService.com

BUSINESS REPLY MAIL

FIRST-CLASS MAIL   PERMIT NO. 717   BUFFALO, NY

POSTAGE WILL BE PAID BY ADDRESSEE

HARLEQUIN READER SERVICE

PO BOX 1341

BUFFALO NY 14240-8571

NO POSTAGE
NECESSARY
IF MAILED
IN THE
UNITED STATES

of photos up on the screen. He hesitated in the darkness, feeling like some creepy voyeur as he took in the delicate line of her neck as she bent over a notebook and scribbled something into its pages.

Damn, he'd thought not seeing her for the past couple of days would have taken some of the sharpness of the ragged edges that had remained after he'd left her bed.

He must have made a sound because she dropped her pen and whipped her head around, her eyes searching the darkness where he stood. Her actions served as the catalyst to make him move forward, to knock gently at her door. Isobel swung the door open and eyed him carefully.

"You're starting to make this a habit, aren't you?"

"May I come in?"

He didn't even fully understand why he was here. All he knew was that he'd felt compelled to come. Now that she was in front of him, he barely knew what to say. His body, on the other hand, had its own agenda. Already he could feel the slow, steady drumbeat of desire through his blood.

She stepped aside and gestured for him to come in. "Can I offer you a drink? A glass of wine or something?"

"Sure," he said, looking at the table where she had a glass of red wine sitting next to her laptop. "Whatever you're having will be fine."

"Are you sure?" Her eyes lit with that habitual spark of waywardness that seemed to linger around her like an aura. "It's not one of yours."

"Tastes like vinegar, does it?" he answered mockingly in return.

"It's actually very good, in my opinion. Mind you, I'm no connoisseur."

Ethan walked over and picked up the bottle, recognizing the New Zealand wine label instantly. "You're right.

Vinegar should never even be mentioned in the same room as this."

Isobel brought him a glass and he poured the ruby liquid into the wide bowl.

"I guess you didn't come here to discuss wine," Isobel said, picking up her own glass and taking a sip.

For a second, Ethan was mesmerized by the tip of her tongue as she ran it along her bottom lip, but then he brought his attention very firmly back to her eyes. There was a challenge in them. One he recognized and to which he instantly felt an answering call.

"No, I didn't. How was your day?"

His question clearly startled her and for a second or two she didn't answer. Eventually, she took a breath and let it out slowly before speaking.

"It was good. And yours? How was your lunch with Shanal?"

"How did you know about that?"

"Was it supposed to be a secret? Cade and I saw you two walking at the botanical gardens. We didn't stop to say hi because he was taking me into Adelaide for the rest of the day."

Ethan felt the obscure urge to apologize for taking Shanal out, but that was ridiculous. He barely knew Isobel. They'd only been acquainted for a handful of days—and their paths would only continue to cross for a few weeks longer before she left The Masters—and him—behind. If he chose to devote his afternoon to a woman who actually intended to stick around, then what right would she have to complain?

"We had a nice afternoon," he settled on saying. "How about you?"

A smile poked at the corners of Isobel's lips. "Cade took me to the apartment."

"He what?"

A gurgle of laughter bubbled from Isobel's mouth. "I thought you'd react like that."

"I'm not reacting," Ethan denied emphatically, tamping down the raw urge to hunt down his younger cousin right here and right now and warn him off Isobel for good.

"He offered me lunch, that's all. He's very good in the kitchen, you know."

Ethan nodded, feeling relief ease through his veins to chase away the irrational urges that had flared so suddenly.

"We're lucky his loyalty to The Masters keeps him here. He's been headhunted by several hotel chains so far, as well as some of the more high-profile restaurants in Sydney and Melbourne."

"It's not stifling him to stay here?" Isobel asked, rolling the rim of her glass across her full lower lip.

Ethan tore his gaze from her mouth. "Stifling him? What makes you say that?"

"You know, keeping him here, working at the café and tasting room instead of letting him stretch his wings elsewhere."

"No one is forcing him to stay, Isobel. We're not quite that feudal."

"Not quite," she agreed. "But you can't deny that he'd do well if he did leave."

"Of course not, but why should he? He's in charge of his own world here. He works with people he knows and trusts—people who care about him and not just about the product he churns out. He's never expressed any desire to be anywhere else."

"Or maybe, because of the expectation to remain here, he's never felt he could."

Ethan narrowed his eyes and looked at her sharply. "Did he ask you to say something to me?"

"No, not at all." Isobel waved a hand in denial. "But he's so talented and still so young. It seems a shame for him to molder away here when the world is, quite literally, his oyster."

"Is that what you think we do here? Molder?"

"Perhaps that wasn't the right word to use," she said quickly. "But you have to admit, it's unusual for one family to stay together like this."

"Unusual, maybe. But not stifling—supportive. We all have a vested interest in how well things go here."

"You more than most."

"What makes you say that?"

Isobel smiled again, the expression making her features lighten from the seriousness of just a moment ago.

"You, of all people, have to ask me that?"

She leaned against the back of the sofa where he'd taken her so urgently two days ago. For the life of him he couldn't get the picture of her out of his mind. His groin ached at the memory. He fisted his empty hand and shoved it in his trouser pocket. It didn't help. Even taking a scouring pad to his memory wouldn't help, he admitted to himself.

Isobel continued when he didn't respond. "It's very clear that the mantle of responsibility here begins and ends with you."

"We all have our part to play," Ethan hedged, oddly unwilling to admit to her that his was the primary role here.

"I'm not used to that. To a setup like you have where all of you are linked by family and work. I suppose I've been on my own for so long that I find it hard to imagine how it could work all together the way you do."

"I guess we're lucky. The business has grown with our strengths. With Cade and Cathleen, for example, they've developed an entirely new side of The Masters, one that complements all the other aspects of our family business, but also one we'd never have considered if they hadn't chosen cuisine and hospitality as part of their studies."

Isobel didn't seem quite ready to agree with him, but at least she didn't seem to wish to argue the point. Instead, she reached for the wine bottle on the table and refilled their glasses.

"Why don't we sit down," she said, putting the bottle on the small coffee table between the sofa and the lazy chair that formed the lounge area of the cottage.

Ethan chose the chair while Isobel curled up on the sofa.

"How are the photos coming along?" Ethan asked, gesturing with his wineglass to the laptop on the dining table.

"Eager to get rid of me?"

"That's not what I said," he answered smoothly, but her response forced him to consider it.

Was he keen for her to leave? Most definitely yes…and then again, no. He didn't like how out of control she made him feel. But then, he didn't like the thought of saying a final goodbye to the passion she stirred in him, either.

"You're still worried about me spilling the beans to Tamsyn about your mother, aren't you?" she asked, cutting straight to the original source of his unease. He did still worry about that. He believed that Isobel liked Tamsyn, that she wouldn't reveal the secret deliberately out of spite. But on the other hand, she seemed uncomfortable with the entrenched structure of their family. As independent as she was herself, Isobel might not believe that he had the right to make the decision to keep the information from his sister, just to protect her.

"It's not your information to share."

"She deserves to know, Ethan." Isobel's voice dropped to a lower pitch, all humor gone.

"Let me be the judge of that."

"I would, but—"

Ethan cut her off. "It's none of your business, Isobel. Leave it alone, okay?"

"It might not have anything to do with me, but it *is* Tamsyn's business. Even you have to accept that."

"Not knowing it hasn't done her any harm for the past twenty-five years. She's managed just fine with my dad and me and our extended family around her. She's not some wounded dove that needs you to campaign on her behalf. She's a strong, beautiful and intelligent woman. Her life doesn't need to be cluttered with questions about a woman who apparently walked away from us both without a backward glance or a second thought. What on earth could knowing she's still alive bring to enrich Tam's life now?"

Isobel took a sip of her wine before answering. "The truth, maybe? Answers as to why she left, why she didn't come back, why she never tried to stay in touch? Have you ever considered that maybe there's more to the story than you know, even now?"

"No." His response was emphatic. "I haven't. Nor do I care to consider it. And as far as Tamsyn is concerned, our mother no longer exists. For now, I'm happy to keep it that way."

"You're wrong, Ethan. You owe it to Tamsyn to let her make up her own mind, make her own choices regarding your mother."

She just wouldn't let it go, would she? Ethan cursed silently. This isn't what he came here for. Hell, he didn't even know himself why he'd sought Isobel's company again but it sure hadn't been for an argument.

"Why are you so hell-bent on making me change my mind?" he asked abruptly.

"Families shouldn't keep secrets," she replied emphatically. "At least not from one another."

A hint of pain showed on her face and his protective instincts flared to the forefront of his mind. What, or more important, *who* had put that sorrow in her soft blue eyes? A parent? A sibling? He had to ask.

"Who kept a secret from you?"

She took her time before answering, and the sudden gleam of moisture in her eyes took him completely by surprise.

"My mother. My father. They conspired to keep mum's illness from me. She suffered from a rare and fatal lung disease, but they never told me once they found out she was sick. She was always just tired or having a bad day. They sheltered me so thoroughly that by the time she was seriously ill, I still barely knew it. Worse, they never gave me a chance to understand *why* she was always unwell."

"How old were you when she died?" he asked softly.

Isobel swiped impatiently at her eyes with one hand and frowned slightly, as if she couldn't bear to show him this weakness. When she continued, her voice was hard, harder than he'd ever heard it and his heart ached a little for the pain she was shielding behind her obvious anger.

"Sixteen. I'd only learned the truth a few months prior. I felt so stupid, as if I'd been deliberately oblivious to her illness. But they never let me understand it. Mum developed complications right at the end. I was only allowed to visit her once in hospital but even then they withheld the truth from me, leading me to believe she'd get well again and come home."

"They were trying to protect you," Ethan said, trying to allay some of her anger and frustration.

"They were keeping a secret from me. Do you honestly think it was fair of them to keep me in the dark like that? I wasn't an idiot, nor was I an infant. I should have had time to understand what her illness could do to her, been given a chance to truly cherish the time we had together.

I never even got to say goodbye to her. Dad arranged for her to be buried without a funeral, without a celebration of her life or the woman she was, or anything."

Tears ran unchecked down Isobel's cheeks now and her voice shook as she continued. "The morning after she passed away, he woke me up and told me she was gone. Then he instructed me to pack a bag with no more than what I could comfortably carry. We went to the airport and that's the last time I saw home. We traveled together until Dad died about four years later. He never really got over Mum's death and I always felt as if he was running away from facing a life without her right up until he passed away."

"Isobel, I'm so sorry you went through that. But Tamsyn's and my situation is different. We're adults now. We've grown up believing one thing all this time. I don't even know what to do with the information about our mother. How can I expect Tamsyn to shoulder that, too?"

"You have to at least give her a chance," Isobel insisted, getting up and finding a paper towel in the kitchenette to dry her tears with. "Like you said, she's an adult. She's quite capable of reaching her own decisions about what to do with the knowledge that your father lied to you both all this time. Is that why you don't want her to know? You don't want her to remember your father any differently than she does now?"

"Maybe," he admitted carefully, surprised at her perceptiveness.

"It won't make her love him any less, you know." Isobel sat back down on the sofa and pulled her knees up under her chin. "For all that my parents kept such an important secret from me, I still love them deep in my heart—I always will. I just wish they'd trusted me with the truth. I was a young adult, but they never respected me enough to share their fears with them. Sheltering me from it all wasn't the best thing for me and it's not the best thing for Tamsyn, either. This is something the two of you should be sharing. You need each other now more than ever."

"I don't agree, but—" he held up a hand when Isobel made to protest once more "—I will give it some more thought. Either way, I need to know I can rely on you to keep the information to yourself. I should never have told you in the first place…."

"But you never expected to see me again. Nor I, you." Isobel sighed. "You know, my mother always loved the poetry of Charles Péguy. Her favorite opening line was '*The faith that I love best, says God, is hope.*' It's what keeps me going—*hope.* Hope that something better, brighter, happier—*anything*—is just around the next corner. I am still angry with my parents for so many reasons for what they did, what I feel as if they stole from me—the chance to make the most of every second with my mother rather than being a bratty teenager. The chance to prepare for a life without her rather than have it thrust upon me. The chance to say goodbye to her and tell her how much I loved her—but I still have hope. Not for a chance to make things right with my parents, obviously. That ship has long since sailed. But I can make a difference for other people. Give them hope, y'know? And you and Tamsyn have that, too. You have a fresh chance with your mother, if you'll only allow yourselves."

"No." His response was absolute. "I don't believe in second chances. I am really very sorry for what you went through, Isobel, but your circumstances are vastly different from ours. And I think, on that note, I should go. We're never going to agree on this issue. Thanks for the wine."

He stood to leave, surprised that Isobel seemingly had

no more to say on the subject. At least until she saw him to the door.

"Trust Tamsyn," she urged as he walked away into the chilled night air. "Trust *her* to know what's the right thing to do about your mother."

"Why can't you just trust me to know what's best for my sister!" he snapped, and turned sharply on his heel to stride away into the darkness.

He simmered with anger all the way back to the house where, unable to help himself, he stood at his window staring down at Isobel's cottage—watching as, one by one, the lights went out, leaving the dwelling in darkness. Why the hell had he gone there? It certainly hadn't been with the intention of arguing about Tamsyn. So what had led him there? Had he wanted to warn her off Cade? Or was it simply to stamp his own possession upon her? Or maybe even to root out the source of his fascination with her so that he could attempt to control it, to control his reaction to her.

Whichever way, he'd failed.

Ten

"These are fabulous!" Tamsyn squealed, her face brightening. "Have you shown Cade and Cathleen?"

"Not yet. I've got an appointment to see them and their restaurant staff later this afternoon."

Isobel leaned back in the chair at Tamsyn's office desk, and watched the slideshow of shots she'd done to date for The Masters new catalog as they slipped across her computer screen. She couldn't help but feel an immense sense of pride in the quality of the work she'd done here. Despite Ethan's remark about mall photos and grumpy babies and toddlers, she felt she did her best work featuring people, and she'd tried to incorporate that here within the guidelines set by Tamsyn and the marketing team.

Even the shots of Raif and his father, tending vines in the distance in what were indisputably her best landscape shots ever, still lent that personal family touch. The body language between the men spoke volumes as to their relationship and how close they were, how much respect they tendered for one another. Of course a lot of the art of that was lost on most people, but it still gladdened her heart to see that she'd captured it, even if from a distance.

Had Ethan and his father been like that? she wondered.

"I love that one." Tamsyn interrupted her reveries. "I know it's the vineyard and all that and the way the sun's dropping over the hills looks fantastic, but I really see Raif and Uncle Edward in that shot. Can we crop it around them more?"

"Sure," Isobel agreed and hit the necessary keys. "Like this?"

"Yeah. Any chance I could have a print of that? I reckon Uncle Edward and Aunt Marianne would love it."

"No problem. I'll put the image on a CD for you and you can have it printed any way you want it." To Isobel's surprise, a look of sadness washed across Tamsyn's face. "Tam? Are you okay?"

Tamsyn gave her a watery smile. "Just missing my dad, I guess."

"That's only natural."

"His death was so sudden, it took all of us by surprise. And now it's just me and Ethan, I feel like I need to hold on to something, you know? We've lost that connection in our lives," she said, gesturing to the cropped photo on the screen. "I don't want to lose it completely by forgetting a thing about Dad. I've tried to talk to Ethan but he won't even discuss him at all. It's like now he's gone, for Ethan, he's really gone. End of story, move on. Dad was the same way, when it came to our mom. I was so little when she died that I barely have any memories of her at all. And now we've lost them both, I...I just wish I had more of them to hold on to."

Tears spilled over her lower lashes and traced silver

streaks down Tamsyn's face. Isobel pushed out of her chair and pulled the other woman into her arms, rocking her silently. She felt Tamsyn's grief like a sword in her gut. It didn't need to be this way. It was wrong of Ethan to withhold the information about their mother. Totally and utterly wrong.

Tamsyn spoke through her tears. "I don't understand the way Ethan's dealing with it. Family means so much to him. But Ethan's just moved on from Dad's death so quickly. I miss Dad, but I don't think my brother does at all. I just don't understand how he can pretend losing our father is nothing to be upset about."

"Everyone grieves differently," Isobel murmured, biting back the words she really wanted to share with Tamsyn.

"I know, and I've read about the different stages of grief. To be honest, I think Ethan is locked in anger—he's mad at Dad for something. What, I don't know. Whether it's the fact that he died so unexpectedly or something else… he just won't talk about any of it with me."

"All you can do is keep trying. He's not the kind of guy who shares his feelings easily, is he?"

A strangled laugh fell from Tamsyn's mouth. "No, he's not. He's always been very staunch, even when we were kids. Some people think he's unsympathetic, but I think it just comes down to the way he shoulders responsibility. He was always the ringleader when we were growing up, and he seemed to think that meant that he wasn't allowed to ever get scared or upset. He wanted to be like Dad—and Dad was always steady and in control. But now he's gone even beyond that. It's as if he's not allowing himself to care at all. He's gotten more distant with our aunts and uncle…and with me. I just wish I knew why."

"You miss your brother—the way he was before your father died," Isobel said with sudden clarity.

"Yes, it's exactly that. We grew up without a mother, we've lost Dad. I feel like I'm losing my brother, too."

"Talk to him," Isobel urged, letting Tamsyn go and grabbing a box of tissues off a nearby shelf. "Make him listen to you. He loves you."

"I know." Tamsyn blew her nose, then turned away from Isobel and wrapped her arms around her body as if shielding herself from her grief. "I just feel like I'm stuck on the outside, y'know? As if I'm on the outside of my own life, looking in like some kid with their face pressed on the glass at Haigh's Chocolates."

"Oh, yeah, that place on the corner of Rundle and King William? I am so that kid!" Isobel laughed at Tamsyn's analogy and tried to lighten the mood, but even so she could still feel her friend's pain emanating off her in waves.

"I think we're all that kid." Tamsyn smiled through her tears. "I love Ethan dearly. He's my rock, and always has been, but he's so determined to be strong for me that he won't let me in. He won't show me what he's really feeling when all I want is to be able to share our grief and help each other work through it."

"Can you talk to Trent about it? After all, you are going to be married to him. He should be helping you through this, too."

An expression Isobel couldn't quite put her finger on appeared in Tamsyn's eyes.

"We're both always so busy with work that we barely see each other. Then, when we do manage to coordinate our schedules and get together, I can see he's stressed with the demands of his job and I really don't want to burden him with anything else."

Just privately, Isobel thought that to be pretty unfair. If you couldn't unload to your partner, who the heck else could you unload to?

Tamsyn sighed and sank into a chair. "I just feel so alone sometimes. I always used to be able to talk to Ethan about virtually anything, and now I really feel like he's holding something back from me."

"He is," Isobel blurted before she could give a second's thought to the ramifications of what she'd begun.

"He what? What do you mean?" Tamsyn asked, her face creased in confusion.

Isobel took in a deep breath. Too late to take back those two insignificant words now. In for a penny, in for a pound, she decided. "He is holding something back from you. You need to ask him about it."

"What? What is it, Isobel? And how come you know about it, if it's such a big secret?"

Oh, God, Isobel thought, she'd really opened a can of worms now. "When I came here that first night, it wasn't the first time I'd met Ethan."

"I knew it!" Tamsyn said. "I knew there was something between you two. I could feel it. He's usually so polite and accommodating when we have a guest and he was so not that way with you. So come on, give up the details."

Isobel cringed inwardly but there was no way she could fudge the truth. Tamsyn deserved that, and more.

"We actually met, by chance, the night before. We, uh, we were intimate with one another."

Tamsyn's eyebrows shot toward her hairline. "You guys had a one-night stand? But Ethan never—"

"Nor do I, but we did. I also never expected to see him again, so coming here and being brought face-to-face like that was a little disconcerting for us both."

The other woman looked at her, assessing what she'd said and narrowing her eyes slightly before speaking. "That's not all, is it? That's not what Ethan's holding back from me."

Isobel closed the short distance between them and squatted on her haunches in front of Tamsyn, reaching for her hands and holding them firmly. "No, it isn't. Ethan confided something in me, something I have no right to tell you but it's something you most definitely deserve to know. Since it appears he has no intention of sharing it with you—and since it's obviously creating a rift between you—I'm going to tell you what he told me."

Tamsyn paled. "It's got to be something awful. Do I really want to know?"

"Maybe not. I know your brother thinks you don't. He's trying to shelter you, keep you from getting hurt. But you need to know, Tam. You deserve the chance to decide how you want to handle this yourself." She squeezed Tamsyn's hands, then spilled the truth.

"Your mother is still alive. Your father hid the truth from you all these years. Ethan only found out that Friday he came to the city. If he's angry at your father, that's why. He's had to battle with the discovery on his own."

For a few moments, Tamsyn was stunned silent. When she finally spoke, Isobel was surprised at the anger in her voice. "He didn't have to, not on his own. Never on his own. He could have had me, if he'd been willing to trust me." Tamsyn's pain was evident in every word she uttered.

"He's your big brother. He just wanted to protect you."

"Oh, don't go making excuses for him." Tamsyn pulled free from Isobel's clasp and stood abruptly, her movement sending her chair skidding backward on the polished wooden floor. "In case either of you hadn't noticed, I'm a grown woman. He had no right to keep that information from me. Neither of you did."

Before Isobel could utter another word, in her own defense or otherwise, Tamsyn was gone, the door slamming behind her. Isobel sat down in the chair that Tamsyn had so rapidly vacated. Her hands shook and her stomach churned uncomfortably. Ethan would be livid. He'd never understand why she'd found it necessary to impart the news he'd been so determined to keep to himself.

A tremor rocked her body at the enormity of what she'd set in motion. What on earth had she done?

Eleven

Ethan left the winery with thunder in his face and murder on his mind. Okay, so maybe murder was taking things just a little too far, but Isobel Fyfe had definitely overstepped the mark. They'd only discussed this very thing last night—he'd reiterated his stance on the matter and yet she'd gone behind his back and told Tamsyn about their mother.

His ears still rang with Tamsyn's vitriolic verbal attack from only moments ago. She'd accused him of all manner of things, including treating her like a child and of pushing her away. He hadn't known what to say. She'd been so angry he decided that it probably didn't matter what he said—nothing would diffuse the situation.

Damn Isobel for sharing news that wasn't hers to tell.

His footsteps echoed sharply on the flagstone path. Isobel had better be at her cottage because what he had to say to her right now did not need an audience and, the way he felt, he wasn't going to hold back even if she was with someone else. Rage roiled inside him as he lifted his fist to hammer on her wooden door which, to his surprise, opened before he could make the first strike.

"I've been expecting you," Isobel said calmly. "Please, come in."

Ethan let his arm drop uselessly to his side. She was expecting him. Well, wasn't that nice?

Isobel turned away from him and moved into the sitting room area, gesturing for him to take a seat.

"I'd rather stand. This won't take long. I've just been with Tamsyn, although I guess you already knew that."

An intense haze of anger dried the words in his throat and he fought to swallow it down. Ethan's fists clenched at his sides and he slowly and deliberately unfurled his fingers, one by one, as he fought to control his fury.

"Why?" he said, when he was finally able to get the growl out of his voice. "Why did you do it?"

To his annoyance, Isobel looked cool and composed.

"Because someone had to and you wouldn't."

"You had no right."

"It's not about my rights—it's about Tamsyn's rights. She deserved to know."

Ethan huffed out a hard breath. "What? Deserved to know that our mother was apparently an alcoholic? One who drove away from here, filled to the gills with wine and with both of us in the car, on her way to meet her lover? A car that she crashed, injuring both of us but allowing her to walk away unscathed—and never come back for us? Do you think Tamsyn is really better off knowing all that?"

He put up a hand as Isobel made to speak. "Don't say a word. You've said more than enough already. You didn't have the full story and you didn't respect my right to withhold it from Tamsyn. I believe now that our father was right to keep the truth from us. We didn't both need to have our childhood memories of our mother tarnished. But now you've taken that choice away from me with your interference."

"Horrible or not, I still believe Tamsyn deserved to know. You might not have wanted to face up to the truth, but she at least had to be given the chance to know what happened and decide for herself how she feels about it."

Isobel stood her ground. Her posture straight and stiff, her blue eyes blazing. She wasn't going to back down and admit she'd been in the wrong and knowing that just spiked his ire even more.

"You don't know any of us well enough to have made that judgment call." Despite the fire raging in his veins his voice was cold and hard. "You're not part of our family, you don't know what we've been through. We were better off without our mother, that much is clear. Now that you've told Tamsyn she's still alive, she has some hare-brained idea that she needs to find her."

"As I would myself, if I had that chance, which is exactly *why* I told Tamsyn. You grew up with your father as your mentor. Who did Tamsyn have?"

"She had all of us—the whole family. We've always been here for each other. Why would she need some drunk who didn't care enough about us to stay? Who actually took money in exchange for agreeing to abandon her children?" he answered scathingly. "Your meddling has created a far bigger problem than having grown up without a mother. Didn't you stop to think beyond the actual words you said? Did the ramifications of Tamsyn knowing only the smallest amount of information not occur to you?"

"She's upset, of course—"

"Upset? *Upset?*" Ethan pushed a hand through his hair in frustration. "Of course she's upset, but worse, she feels abandoned now on top of everything else. And she wants to know why. She's a determined young woman, Isobel. She won't rest until she knows the full truth behind what happened and, dammit, she doesn't need that cluttering up her life right now."

Isobel eyed him carefully. "She doesn't? Or *you* don't? Be honest with yourself, Ethan. You don't need this as a complication in your life. You were quite happy to just trawl on in your own private kingdom, maintaining the status quo. Don't you remember your mother? Don't you remember the good times with her? Tamsyn was too young for any of that but now she still has a chance to learn about her and, if she's lucky, to forge a relationship with her. Yet you still think you had the right to stand in her way of happiness."

"*What* happiness? Our mother abandoned us. Do you think she really wants Tamsyn to walk back into her life now? What happens when Tamsyn tracks her down and gets rejected—when instead of barely remembering a mother who died, she gets to have crystal-clear memories of her mother telling her to her face that she doesn't want her?"

He was viciously pleased to see Isobel flinch at that, but she still didn't back down. "You can't know that will happen. And even if it does, all you can do is be there for her. Tell her the whole truth, and then help her deal with it. Let her help *you* deal with it. You can't protect her by shutting her out. She feels like an outsider in her own home. Did you know that?"

Ethan felt her words suck the anger out from deep inside him, leaving behind a void of darkness and hurt. He shook his head abruptly.

"I suppose she told you that during your little heart-to-heart?" he bit out.

"She did. That's why I told her about your mother. Once everything's out in the open, you won't have to exclude her anymore. She can finally understand what's going on."

Silence stretched out between them until Ethan groaned. "I wish I'd never met you."

He watched the impact of his words upon her dispassionately, noted the tightening of her lips, the paleness that replaced the natural warmth in her cheeks.

"It was inevitable, Ethan—Tamsyn finding out about your mother. It was going to happen eventually."

He shook his head. "I want you to leave."

"I told you before and I'll tell you again. My contract isn't with you. I'm not going until my job is done."

"If you had any decency, you'd go."

"It's because of my integrity that I'm staying. Besides, Tamsyn needs someone in her corner right now who's willing to be honest with her. I will not desert her."

Ethan stared hard into her eyes. She didn't so much as blink, meeting his gaze in a full-on challenge.

"Just stay out of my way," he growled.

"That's going to be hard to do," Isobel said. "We have the wine-tasting shoot this week. Can we at least be civil to one another?"

"Civil, you say? I don't feel terribly civil right now. I can arrange for one of the others to be there in my stead."

She shook her head. "No, that won't do. The focus of the new brochures is the Masters family ethos. As head winemaker and new head of the family, you have to be involved."

To his surprise, Isobel stepped closer and laid one hand on his chest. "You're a good man, Ethan Masters. I know you love Tamsyn, I know you wanted to do what you thought was best for her."

"And yet you still went ahead and told her anyway.

We'll never be able to go back, Tamsyn and I. Nothing will ever be the same."

"Change can be a good thing."

Isobel's hand dropped away from him and, as much as he hated to admit it, he felt its loss immediately. He didn't want to be that weak—to allow her to affect him this way. His response, when it came, was sharp and clear.

"I hope for your sake it is. You say that Tamsyn is your friend and that you wanted to help her, so if this ends up blowing up in our faces, with our mother leaving Tamsyn feeling even more rejected and betrayed, then you 'helped' her right into a whole new world of heartbreak. A world *I* tried to protect her from ever entering."

Before she could respond, he spun on his heel and stalked back out of the cottage. The fury that had driven him there had abated but it had been replaced by a cold, hard anger that sat like a leaden ball in his gut.

"Well, that went well," Isobel said to the empty room after Ethan had left.

She sank down onto the sofa and hugged her arms around her. She'd known he'd be angry but she'd expected a full-on explosion of it—not the intensely controlled version Ethan had brought to her just now. It made her begin to wonder if Ethan had come to terms with the news about Ellen Masters himself. As she turned the thought over in her mind, it occurred to her that he probably hadn't even had time to properly grieve his father's death, either.

Being as controlled as he was—as responsible and conservative as he was—he had to be undergoing a massive internal struggle with himself. Her heart ached for him. She knew what that struggle felt like, should—in an ideal world—be able to help him with this. But their entire relationship, if you could call it such a thing, had been flashes of passion interspersed with flashes of disagreement. It was the original push-me-pull-you type of attraction she'd never understood in others. Didn't understand in herself now, either, to be honest.

Isobel looked across the room and out the picture window that faced the vineyard. The Masters was all about stability, longevity and growth. All of which formed strong foundations in their family. She'd undermined that stability by taking it upon herself to tell Tamsyn what she had today.

She still believed she'd been right to do it—but at what cost to everyone else? Ethan was right that Tamsyn would be very vulnerable when she confronted her mother. If the meeting went badly and the rift was still in place between her and her brother, would she even be willing to turn to her family for comfort? The thought of that, more than anything, sat very heavy in her heart right now.

She couldn't regret what she'd done. But she could ache, with all her heart, over the pain it had caused for both Ethan and Tamsyn.

The next few days proved busy, a fact for which she was grateful. Tamsyn appeared to be none the worse for the revelation about her mother, although Isobel noted that from time to time her attention would wander, her expression become pensive. Personally, Isobel felt that Trent should be very strongly supporting Tamsyn right now but he remained as scarce as he'd been through the duration of her stay to date. When Isobel pressed Tamsyn about this, her friend merely brushed her concern aside, saying he was busy in the city and that she was okay.

When the morning of the wine-tasting shoot dawned, Isobel rose early, her stomach tied in knots. She scowled at her reflection as she brushed her teeth at the bathroom mirror, reminding herself she was a professional and would continue to behave that way no matter how distant or rude Ethan might be.

Ethan. God, the very thought of him sent a spear of longing through her body, making every sense come alive. She had it bad, but infatuation was like that. They'd barely seen each other since he'd confronted her here at the cottage, but even if they hadn't had their falling-out, she doubted she would have gotten much of his time. He was incredibly busy at the winery, pulling long hours with his team as the harvest from their reserve block arrived. New barrels had been brought in and even though Isobel had taken shots of the entire process, Ethan had kept his distance from her.

Today, though, it would be only the two of them. The new brochure would feature each family member in their role at the vineyard. The photo of Raif and his father, Edward, working in such obvious unity had been the family's pick for the vineyard part of the operation. Tamsyn in her office, her wall planner filled behind her, a phone to her ear and her day planner in her hand, had been designated for the accommodation and events along with a surprisingly poignant photo Isobel had taken of the bride and groom during bridezilla's special day last weekend. Cade and Cathleen together with the chef at the restaurant had photographed well in a lighthearted moment that had been an absolute joy to capture. Now it was Ethan's turn.

Isobel checked the smaller daypack she carried with her when she worked, making sure her camera batteries were fully charged and that she had additional memory cards if she needed them. Ethan was delightfully photogenic, she'd discovered in the surreptitious shots she'd taken of him to date. The camera loved the sculpted lines of his face and the way the light fell upon his bone structure. An all-too-familiar ache throbbed low in her belly, forcing her to remind herself that for today, he was only a subject. One to be captured in the course of his work—that was all.

Ethan was prepared and waiting for her at the winery when she arrived. She checked her watch quickly—no, she wasn't late and yet he had that look about him as if he'd been waiting for her for some time. She cast her eye across the setting he'd created—the bentwood chairs set at a crisp-white-linen-covered round table with a row of barrels behind them and the handcrafted stone walls visible as a backdrop. The lighting was to be augmented with strategically placed spotlights that Isobel had hired specifically for this shoot, and she could see them standing off to one side.

"Good morning," Ethan said as she drew closer.

Isobel felt an indefinable frisson ripple down her spine. So he was going for civilized today. She could live with that.

"Good morning. Thank you for setting up in advance today."

He nodded in acknowledgment. "Do you need a hand with the spots?"

Isobel considered the lighting in the area. It was dim, but had a distinct ambience that lent itself well to the solemnity of the process she knew was about to be unveiled to her camera. If she made the right adjustments it was possible she might not need the spotlights after all.

"I think I'll leave them for now," she said. "If you could sit there, at the table for a moment, I'll do a few test shots and see."

Ethan did as she bid without comment. Isobel moved around him, her camera poised and ready for action. The minute she caught him in her viewfinder, her stomach clenched. He was so incredibly beautiful in the most masculine kind of way. A persistent buzz of awareness set up deep inside her but she fought to ignore it. Taking a step back, she scrolled through the photos she'd just taken.

"Stay where you are," she instructed. "We're going to need additional light after all."

She fussed with the spots, taking more shots, until with a grunt of satisfaction, she knew she had the right juxtaposition of light and shadow.

"Okay, we're ready to roll," she said, lifting her camera to her eye again. "Now, just start talking and leading me through the wine-tasting process. Use two glasses on the table, as if you have company."

She waited for Ethan to move. He appeared to hesitate, as if to say something, but then he reached for the gold-labeled Shiraz on the table. Instinctively, Isobel began to shoot.

"Wine tasting is an adventure that engages your senses," Ethan started, his voice deep and smooth and sending a thrill of delight through Isobel that she couldn't ignore. "It's more than just taste, although taste is vitally important and highly individual. It also involves you visually, engages your olfactory senses and plays on your emotions and memories at the same time."

Isobel's finger worked the shutter button unconsciously as Ethan opened the wine and gently poured a sample into each of two empty glasses on the table. His voice provided a background commentary that stroked her senses to boiling point, making it more and more difficult with each shot to keep her focus on her subject and not on what his passion for his subject was, in kind, doing to her.

Ethan lifted one of the glasses from the table, angling the bowl slightly away from him, and began explaining about color and tone. Isobel was so caught up in his words that she forgot she was supposed to be merely a silent observer, and found herself speaking up.

"To be honest," Isobel interjected, "My wine expertise has always come down to what I like the taste of and how much I like that taste. I've never really stopped to consider color or density."

Ethan turned and gave her a smile that just about made her toes curl. Clearly, in this moment, his animosity had been forgotten. "Then you're seriously missing out. Put the camera down and come here. Try it."

"But I thought you only had an hour for me today."

He shrugged. "So I'll have to make up time somewhere else. This is important. The better you understand the method, the better the photos will be, right?"

Isobel didn't answer, she merely placed her camera down on the table and sat opposite Ethan. She felt absurdly pleased when he gave her a nod of approval.

"Let's see if we can't instill a better appreciation of the process of tasting wine, hmm?" he said.

"You make it sound like a ritual," she commented, picking up her glass and doing as he'd done earlier, tilting it and studying the color and clarity with the same absorption she usually reserved only for her proofs.

"It is, in a way. And there's nothing wrong in making a ceremony out of it, in showing our appreciation for the work that's gone into bringing this bottle to the table all the way from the vine."

Ethan's enthusiasm for his subject shone through in his every gesture and every word. If at all possible, it made him even more attractive to her, and as he continued to lead her through the formalities of using her senses to see, smell and taste the wine he'd chosen for the shoot she felt herself falling for him just that bit more. Ethan the vintner was a far cry from Ethan the authoritative brother and family head. He was just as deliberate and in control, but it felt easier and more natural to let him take the lead in this arena where he was so clearly an expert…and where he was using his expertise to enhance the pleasure she'd find in the experience. As she tasted her wine and allowed the carefully formulated final product roll around in her mouth, she wondered briefly what it would be like to see him year-round—to observe him work through every step of his magical process, turning harvested fruit into a sensation of aromas and flavors that gave her a new appreciation for his art.

See him year-round? What on earth was she thinking? She was transient and she liked it that way. Seeing a man like Ethan Masters year-round would mean staying in his world, because he certainly wasn't the kind of man to uproot himself to live in hers. A man like him had roots that went deeper in the soil at The Masters than those of the vines that striated the fields around them. He wouldn't accept anything less than a permanent, lifelong commitment.

She didn't do permanent. Had never wanted to.

A shocking afterthought penetrated deep into her heart. Until now, perhaps.

Twelve

To give herself some distance from her thoughts, Isobel deliberately set her glass down on the pristine white cloth and reached for her camera again. As she did so, a drop of wine from the rim of her glass tracked down the outside of the bowl and along the stem, spreading onto the base until it leaked into the finely woven linen, leaving a stain.

As she had with her presence here.

Ethan liked everything neat and organized, with every piece tucked into place. Isobel brought mess and chaos with her everywhere she went. She'd brought it to Ethan's life. The thought came to her sharp and swift, and it hurt. She still believed she'd done the right thing by sharing with Tamsyn the information. But only now did she fully appreciate the repercussions of what she'd done. Only now, when she really considered what it might be like to be part of his family, did she think of the damage she might have done to all of them by opening the door between Tamsyn and the secret the rest of her family had made the decision to keep.

This family, these people, they were intertwined with one another just as much as the vines were on the frames they grew along. Each dependent on the other for its success, its support. And she'd potentially undermined that.

It just went to show that she was better off on her own. Whenever she spent time with a strong family or community, it only went to prove to her that she had no idea how to belong. No idea how to be anything other than alone.

"I'm sorry, Ethan," she blurted.

"For the spot on the cloth? Don't worry. We've seen far worse."

"No." She shook her head. "Not that. I mean for telling Tamsyn. I know you had your reasons for keeping the news about your mother to yourself. Whether I agreed with them or not I shouldn't have interfered."

Ethan sighed and rose from the table. "No, you shouldn't have interfered, but I won't accept your apology, either."

He wouldn't? A sudden spurt of anger flared and, just as quickly, extinguished inside of her. He wouldn't. No, of course not. She was the outsider here. The interloper who'd well and truly set a cat among the pigeons.

"That's okay, I understand," she managed to say through lips that felt as thick and unresponsive as rubber. "Look, I think I have everything I need here today. Let me run these through my computer and I'll forward you a selection to choose from for your brochure."

"Isobel, wait."

His voice was a command, not a request. It was so like him, she thought with a rueful twinge of recognition.

"You want me to take some more shots?"

"No." He brushed her question aside with an impatient movement of his hand.

A hand that had done exquisite things to her body. A hand that had left her panting and demanding more—which was exactly what he'd given. A tiny shudder rippled through her. This was torture. Very different from what had been threatened toward her before she'd vacated the country she'd last been in, but equally as devastating emotionally.

She stood silently, awaiting his next move and wishing he would get to whatever it was that he wanted to say. Once he was done, maybe he'd finally let her go to gather her scattered nerves back to some semblance of order again. But his words, when they came, knocked the air straight out of her lungs.

"I owe *you* an apology."

She didn't know what to say, how to act. She let instinct take over.

"No, you don't. I was in the wrong. I acted without really thinking it through."

He mustered a half smile. "I can't say I'm thrilled with the way you went about it, but you were still right. If anyone deserved the full story about our parents it was Tamsyn. I should have told her from the start, when I'd found the discrepancy in my father's personal accounts. If not then, certainly when I found out that our mother was still living."

"I...I don't know what to say."

It was a new sensation for Isobel. Normally she had no trouble blurting out whatever came next in her mind. But this? An apology from this incredibly strong and proud man? She knew how hard it must have been for him to back down like this.

"Then don't say anything. Just listen. Tamsyn and I had a long talk last night. She's still mad at me, and rightly so, but I accept that I was being overprotective. I do still try to shelter her—she *is* my little sister, after all, and I doubt my need to shield her from things will ever go away entirely. But she's an adult—one who had every right, just as you said, to know what I knew. We've discussed it all. Our memories of our mother, the little we got out of our father, the information the solicitor gave me—everything."

"I'm glad you guys could sort it out," Isobel said, gathering her things together to hide her awkwardness.

To her surprise, his hands closed around hers, halting her in her actions. How on earth had he moved so fast? He drew her round to face him.

"Isobel, I am sorry for the way I spoke to you. I've been angry since the day I met you—struggling to come to terms with my father's death, with my additional responsibilities here, with the awful truth he kept from Tam and me all those years. I began to associate you with that emotion, and it wasn't fair." His mouth quirked into a crooked smile, one that made her heart somersault in her chest before he continued. "I'm not proud to admit it, but I needed you that first night to take me away from all of that—to wipe things from my mind. By the morning, when you'd gone, I felt as though I had it all under control again. Then, when you turned up here, it just brought my vulnerability back to me. Being weak isn't something that sits comfortably on my shoulders."

"Believe me, whatever pleasure or escape you got from us being together, I got that, too."

"Escape? What do you need to escape from, Isobel?"

He lifted a hand to move a strand of hair from where it had fallen across her cheek. His touch sent an instant line of fire searing across her skin.

For a minute she thought of the atrocities she'd so recently left behind her. The ones she still felt a moral burden to bring to public awareness through her blog and, with luck, more gallery showings worldwide. This world here at The Masters was so far removed from the day-to-day existence she'd come to accept as normal that, by contrast, it was almost a fantasy come true.

But whose fantasy? She hadn't stood still long enough in the past ten years to even begin to remember what it was like to be rooted in one place. To call somewhere home. And she didn't want to, she reminded herself with a hard mental shake. No matter how compelling the impetus to do otherwise.

"Isobel?" Ethan prompted.

She shook her head. "Nothing. Just…nothing."

"Am I forgiven?" he asked, his dark eyes boring into hers as if willing it to be so.

"Of course," she answered as lightly as she could manage. "But you must forgive me, too."

"Done," he agreed.

Isobel pulled her hands from his and stepped back. "Right, now that's settled, I'd better get back to work."

She felt flustered, his behavior today surprising her more than she cared to admit—showing a side of him that she hadn't envisioned.

"Don't let me hold you back," Ethan replied, turning to the table and recapping the wine bottle. "Here, take this back to your cottage and when you try it, think about what we went over."

Isobel very much doubted she'd ever be able to think about anything or anyone else when she touched wine again, but she accepted the bottle and then collected her camera bag and left the winery. Outside the autumn sunshine was clear and bright, quite a contrast to the controlled environment she'd just left and, she realized, a perfect analogy for her and Ethan. His world was controlled by season and longevity, security and routine. Her world was full of light and air and impermanence. They didn't belong together. Aside from a physical synchronicity that transcended all others, they were complete and utter opposites.

But if that was the case, why did it hurt so much to think about leaving here, leaving him?

Ethan returned from dinner with Shanal feeling completely out of sorts. Despite his overtures, she'd shown no interest in developing their relationship any further than their existing friendship. He'd seeded their conversation with hints about her hopes for the future, her dreams. Marriage hadn't figured in there at all. And then there'd been the lack of physical contact or even chemistry between them. Sure, they'd talked long into the evening about their work, but he knew that if a marriage between them was to work, they needed more. They needed some compatibility beyond inquiring minds and similar interests.

Yet every time he thought about compatibility, a different face swam into view. A face framed with sun-kissed blond hair. A face with blue eyes, not green. He'd felt better for apologizing to Isobel and hoped the truce between them would dull the edge of the wild infatuation that had plagued him from the moment he'd first seen her. He'd sworn to himself he'd keep his hands off her from now on. It was too dangerously addictive being around her.

Fortunately, creating distance between them at The Masters had proven quite straightforward as she threw herself into finishing the assignment. They'd crossed paths only briefly since she'd done the tasting shoot, acknowledging one another's presence with little more than a nod or a wave in passing. Their dealings were now confined to email as he'd approved her selection of proofs to be dealt with by their marketing department.

He knew she'd be leaving soon, very soon. It was a

relief to know he didn't have to spend every waking minute wondering if he'd see her or catch a reminder of her scent.

Ethan garaged his car and made his way up to his bedroom, crossing the floor swiftly to draw his drapes closed. As he did each night, however, he paused at the window. His eyes were inexorably drawn to Isobel's cottage. The interior lights burned until late every night. Either she was a complete night owl or she had about as much trouble sleeping as he did. He closed the drapes with a sharp snap and got ready for bed, forcing his thoughts to turn to Shanal Peat again.

What was it about the two of them that didn't spark? he wondered as he lay in the dark. He'd thought it would be so simple. Well, he'd make it work somehow. He just had to. He had the future of his entire family network to consider and ensuring its stability was one of his many responsibilities. Someone like Shanal was perfect.

And if he told himself often enough, he might just believe it.

But as the hours ticked over and sleep remained elusive, he found his thoughts straying in a different direction. One that lay only a couple of hundred meters from him right now. One that was completely wrong for him and his plans for the future on so many levels he shouldn't even be thinking of her at all.

Ethan rolled over and focused on making his body relax, emptying his mind, breathing deep—and then starting with his toes and working up his body, clenching and releasing muscles until he all but melted into the surface of his mattress. Then an image of Isobel flicked into his mind again. Just like that he was taut as a bow once more. Taut and aching and thinking all kinds of inappropriate thoughts for a man who was attempting to woo a different woman altogether.

What kind of man did that make him? Certainly not one he was proud to be. All his life he'd striven for excellence, worked tirelessly for his family's and, more important, his father's respect. And he'd earned it. He'd basked in their pleasure in his achievements, at first academically and then later on with the wines he'd produced to many international accolades.

He'd done it all for them but he'd done it for himself, too. He enjoyed the ride, the challenges, the success. Why couldn't he succeed at this? Why did his friendship with Shanal lack the vital catalyst that pushed a relationship past amity and into passion?

And why couldn't he get his mind off a woman who was wrong for him in every way? She was a free spirit, while he was bound by a hundred different ties. He thrived on responsibility and commitment while she ran the other way. He wanted to spend his life at The Masters, contributing to his family's legacy, while by all indications, she couldn't get away fast enough. And yet somehow, Isobel challenged him on every level—mentally and physically. He didn't want to want her like this but she was now embedded in his psyche.

He got out of bed with a frustrated growl and went through to his bathroom for a glass of water. Something, he hoped, that would slake the thirst that made him crave so much more than a long draw of cool liquid.

She'd be leaving The Masters soon, probably even leaving Australia, and that was a very good thing, he told his hazy reflection in the moonlit en suite. A very good thing, indeed.

But the thought of never seeing her again made his body ache and turned his mind to the two nights they'd shared. He wanted more. He wanted her. He wanted that sensation of having his senses scattered to the wind, he wanted to take risks and do crazy things with her. He wanted, even for only that briefest moment, to be wonderfully and truly happy again. To forget the responsibilities and pressures that confined him and to give himself over fully to the moment.

He wanted Isobel Fyfe.

Thirteen

"Ethan, you have to go to the awards ceremony. You can't possibly think of sending someone else."

Tamsyn had been reminding him of the upcoming wine awards ceremony for days now and he'd been ignoring each reminder deliberately. He knew he had an amazing team but he also hated to leave the property at this stage of the winemaking process. The reserve chardonnay was about to head into its secondary fermentation and bulk aging in oak barrels, while the Shiraz was already into its malo-lactic fermentation stage.

Sure, he could delegate a lot of the testing that needed to take place at this point—it was how he'd been trained by his father and how his father had been trained before him, after all. If you didn't share and, in some cases, relinquish responsibility, no one learned anything of real value along the way. The family often teased him about the strangle-hold he kept on operations and his pedantic methods, but they worked. After all, wasn't that why The Masters was up for this most recent award in the first place? Quality was everything.

"Ethan? Are you even listening to me?" Tamsyn persisted.

"Of course I'm listening to you. Will you come with me?"

"I wish I could, you know that. But this weekend is bridezilla's parents' surprise anniversary and vow renewal service." His sister pulled a face that left no doubt as to how eager she was to see the back of the coming weekend. "Why don't you take someone else?"

"Hmm, I wonder if Shanal is free?" he pondered out loud.

"Shanal? I was thinking more along the lines of Isobel." Tamsyn gave him a pointed look.

"Isobel?" His senses went on high alert at the very thought of her.

"Why not? Maybe she could take some photos, as well. Marketing will be able to use them, if not in the new brochure then certainly for other publicity releases for the vintage. I can check with her if you like."

Ethan stroked his chin thoughtfully. If he took Isobel, he knew the awards ceremony would be very much the last thing on his mind. "Let me check with Shanal first."

"Really? Ethan, she's lovely and she's a wonderful friend but why are you doing this?"

"What are you talking about?"

"Why are you ignoring what you could have with Isobel to chase after Shanal, who we both know you don't care about in that way?"

"Tamsyn—" he started to protest but his sister cut him off.

"No, don't fob me off. We've learned the hard way how

precious things are in life. How special relationships can be. I know you like Shanal, and she's lovely, but she's your friend, not your lover. You can't create what isn't there. With Isobel I know you have that special something. Can't you just give it a try?"

"Look, you're on the wrong track. Isobel and I... We're not suited. It wouldn't work out in the long term."

"Damn the long term!" Tamsyn's outburst startled him. "What about how she makes you *feel?* Think about it, Ethan. Life isn't just a series of processes season in and season out. Sometimes you have to roll with change, exercise your senses, allow yourself to take a walk on the wild side. Do what feels right in the moment instead of sticking to the plan come what may."

There were tears in his sister's eyes. "What's going on, Tamsyn? This is about more than who I invite to the awards, isn't it?"

"Of course it is. I don't know about you, but I don't feel like I can just trot along on my merry little life path the way I used to anymore. Things have changed. We need to learn to change with them. Since Dad died I've been thinking a lot about my life and my future. I don't know if I want the same things anymore. I don't think, if you're really honest with me and with yourself, you do, either. And I have questions that I no longer have the answers for. Don't you? Don't you want to know more about Mum, about why she left, about why she stayed away? About why Dad never spoke about her again or let her see us?

"Things have changed now that I know she's alive. I can't pretend everything's the same and just trundle along as if all is business as usual. I don't feel as if I can move forward again until I know the answers to those questions. They're important to me. You should be considering what's really important to you, too."

She turned and left his office before he could reply, tension radiating from her body in waves. It upset him to see her like this. Tamsyn was usually so centered, so level. Always the one to smooth troubled waters and to make sure that everyone was happy. Their father had called her "his biddable child" because she'd always do whatever was expected of her with a smile on her face. He knew she'd still deliver on everything that was expected of her, but at what cost to herself?

Damn, he wished she was still his baby sister that he could still guard against the things that would upset her, but he'd accepted he could no longer do that. She was an adult and had long since earned the right to stand on her own two feet. All he could do was make certain she knew she had his backing if she needed it, as he had hers. Which brought him back to what she'd said just now. About considering what was important to him.

The Masters, most definitely, and everyone associated with it—but even as he thought it, his mind drifted to a slender waif of a woman. One with lightly tanned skin, clear blue eyes and hair the color of sunshine after a spring rain.

He was on his feet and heading out of his office before he could double think this. Tamsyn was right. His time with Isobel was short. He needed to make the most of it.

And he wouldn't let himself think about how soon it would come to an end.

"Are you sure this is a good idea?" Isobel asked as she tightened the straps on her pack.

"No."

Ethan's reply was succinct and made her look up and do a double take at the expression on his face.

"I thought we weren't going to—"

"We weren't."

"But we're—"

"We are."

"Okay." She breathed out on a long breath and lifted her pack to walk out of the cottage toward Ethan's car. "Are we staying in the apartment again?"

His lips firmed as if he was weighing up his response. "Yes, unless you'd rather stay at a hotel?"

"No, I'd rather be at the apartment. I liked it there," she answered with a smile that felt both slightly shy and un-ashamedly bold at the same time.

He was different today. In fact, he'd been different from the moment he'd asked her if she'd like to be his plus one at the awards evening. She'd basically wrapped up all her work at The Masters, with the exception of a shoot of Cade's latest dessert creation, which Cathleen had insisted on including in their feature. Theoretically, she was a free spirit once again. Free to travel whenever and wherever she wanted to.

The human rights issues were calling her again. The idyll here in South Australia had been an opportunity to recharge her batteries but she needed to get back to work—real work—very soon.

She had to be honest with herself, though. There had been a very definite hold on her here. A hold which began and ended with the man walking at her side—the man who set her senses alight with no more than a glance. The pros-pect of even just one more night with him made her senses vibrate with a keenness she knew she ought to control bet-ter, but for the life of her, simply didn't want to.

The ride into Adelaide was smooth and swift and Isobel found herself looking for specific landmarks on the way through. Landmarks that led them closer to the apartment.

Ethan spoke only occasionally on the journey into the city but he seemed relaxed, happy even.

When he pulled into the underground parking at the apartment tower and rolled the car into its space, he suddenly reached across the compartment and took her hand.

"We've got time. Come on."

"Time? For what?" She felt the beginnings of a smile tug at her lips.

"You'll see." He smiled back and let her hand go, reaching across her to open her car door. "Come on. Let's not waste a second."

This side of Ethan was different from the ones she'd seen before. He was more carefree. And the expression on his face, all heat and intent, was making her stomach somersault in anticipation of what he had in mind. Ethan was out of the car and grabbing their things from the trunk before she had even unclipped her seat belt.

"Come on, lazybones," he chided playfully. "Let's go."

She did as he said, catching up with him as he began to walk toward the elevator without so much as a glance back at her. He hit the remote lock and she heard the car's electronic system engage just as she caught up to him.

The ride up in the elevator was mercifully swift. Isobel's skin felt tight, too tight for her body, and the light abrasion of her clothing reminded her with every step of the featherlight touch of Ethan's fingertips upon her. By the time the doors opened in the foyer of the apartment she thought she might explode with the tension that gripped her.

Ethan stepped out of the elevator and dropped their bags on the floor with one movement, then reached for her in another. She was plastered against his body before her thoughts could catch up with her actions. His erection pressed hard against her, his mouth lowered and caressed hers softly before taking her lips in a kiss that all but blew her mind.

She reached up and hooked her arms around the back of his neck, her fingers tangling in the short strands of his hair and pulling him toward her. She couldn't get close enough, taste him enough. She swept her tongue gently over his lower lip before catching it lightly between her teeth, suckling against the soft flesh before releasing him again. He shuddered against her, grinding his hips against hers, sliding his thigh between her jean-clad legs and hitching her up slightly.

Instinctively, her pelvis tilted and she felt the jolt of energy that radiated from her core. She moaned aloud only to have the sound snatched from her mouth as he kissed her again, this time deeper, harder, stronger than before. His hands slid down her body, cupping her buttocks and lifting her higher. She hitched her legs around his waist, holding on to him for dear life as he began to walk them both down the hall, never taking his lips from her for one second.

Finally, blissfully, she felt a bed at her back. She reached for the fastening of his jeans, her fingers shaking as she undid the metal buttons and shoved the denim off his hips and down the top of his thighs. He did the same, albeit with a little more finesse—taking her G-string briefs with her jeans and hooking off her slip-on shoes in a modicum of movement.

Isobel reached for him, her fingers closing around his length through his boxer briefs, stroking him through the cotton, reaching lower to cup his balls and squeeze lightly as he dragged a condom from the bedside cabinet. He was sheathed in seconds, sliding inside her in less.

Their tempo was frantic, her heart beating so fast in her chest she thought she might expire. At last, with a deep

thrust, Ethan pushed her body over the edge of desperation and into a realm of feeling so rich and so divine she
felt tears slip from the corners of her eyes. He collapsed
against her, shoving her deep into the mattress as his body
pulsed with his own release.

She lay beneath him, relishing the weight of his body
pinning her to the bed, still enraptured by the heights of
responsiveness he drew from her body. She wrapped her
arms tight around his waist, not wanting this moment,
this closeness to end. Ethan nuzzled her neck, nipping her
skin lightly and sending another ripple coursing through
to her core. She clenched her inner muscles tight around
him, and felt an answering reaction in his own body, that
involuntary throb of sensation.

"Let's blow off this thing tonight and just stay here," he
said against her throat. "I have tortured myself with denial
of you for far too long. Let's not waste another minute."

She laughed, tempted to agree to his outrageous sug-
gestion, but the accolade he was nominated for tonight was
major industry recognition. She wanted to see him win,
wanted to share in his success.

"We have the rest of the night after the dinner and
awards."

"No, it's not enough," he said, pressing a line of kisses
around the neckline of her blouse. "It'll never be enough."

"What if I promise that if you win, I'll…"

She whispered something in his ear.

"Only if I win?"

"Well, maybe if you don't win, too, but only if we go
and I get those photos Tamsyn insisted on."

He groaned and rested his forehead on hers. "You drive
a hard bargain, but okay. I agree. Let's go shower."

He withdrew from her body and stood up, grabbing her
hands and pulling her up with him. She laughed again as

he kicked off his shoes and the jeans that had settled at his ankles. She felt so relaxed, so unbelievably happy.

So very much in love.

Fourteen

No. She couldn't be. Not in love. She'd never loved a man, not like this. The realization was exhilarating and terrifying in equal measure. No, cancel that, she thought. It was quite simply terrifying. She didn't love. Love meant attachment. Love meant being with someone forever. She didn't do forever. She did change—a kaleidoscope of people, places, lives.

But this feeling, this overwhelming reaction that filled her heart and her mind—it was different from anything else she'd ever felt before. It exhilarated her, but it terrified her at the same time.

Emotionally numb, Isobel allowed Ethan to lead her to the bathroom where he led them into a massive multihead shower and began to soap up her body. The slick feel of his lathered hands on her skin was a welcome distraction to the shattered thoughts that splintered through her mind. She grabbed a metaphorical hold of the desire that began to grow within her, allowing Ethan's touch to stoke that fire so that it consumed all thought of anything else. When he knelt before her, placing his lips and mouth at her core, doing unspeakably creative things to her with his tongue, she let herself ride the waves until he coaxed her over the edge and into oblivion, leaving her shaking and weak, barely able to stand—definitely unable to think.

The rest of the evening passed in a blur. She knew she did the right things, went through the right motions, took the right photos, but inside she was still in shock. How had she allowed him under her radar? How had he inveigled his way into her heart?

In the aftermath of her mother's death and her father's quest to run from his grief for the rest of his life, Isobel had sworn she would never let anyone matter that much to her. She never wanted another soul to have that power to inflict hurt or sorrow on her life. She never wanted to be dependent on another for her happiness.

The way she chose to live was her protection. Looking at her world through a lens, but not necessarily being involved on a deeper scale with it. Oh, sure, she knew people argued that if she didn't empathize with her subjects, or at the very least feel some sense of responsibility toward them, that she wouldn't enjoy the success she'd had to date, and they weren't wrong. She let herself feel, let herself care, but never let herself get truly attached.

Isobel watched Ethan across the table where they'd been seated upon arrival at the awards ceremony. He looked up for a moment, as if aware of her gaze, and gave her a small secret smile. The look in his eyes made her breath catch in her throat. As he held her gaze she felt her nipples tighten beneath the dress she wore, one that Tamsyn had loaned her and which made her eyes look bluer than blue and her skin become almost luminescent. She smiled in return. It was all she was capable of here in this room filled with people and noise and the clatter of cutlery on fine china. But when she got Ethan alone, oh, yes, then she'd show him exactly what that look did to her, and she'd do it to him, too.

She noted the exact second her intent reflected in her eyes, the flare of acceptance, of challenge, in his own. His smile deepened and she felt as if time stood still as he made his excuses to the people he was talking with and rose from the table. He was at her side in a moment, his warm hand on her bare shoulder.

"Had enough for tonight?" he asked as he bent down slightly, his breath warm in her ear and sending a thrill of excitement through her.

"Not nearly enough," she replied, reaching for the small beaded bag Tamsyn had also loaned her and rising as he pulled out her chair.

"Let's not waste another second, then, hmmm?" he said as he tucked her hand in the crook of his elbow.

They were delayed a few times by people wanting to congratulate Ethan on his latest gold medal success, but the accolades appeared to wash over him. Tension radiated from his body, transferring itself to her in waves.

As the valet brought Ethan's car around the front of the reception center she asked him, "Did you enjoy yourself this evening?"

"Not as much as I enjoyed thinking about the rest of tonight with you."

She laughed, the sound a gurgle of joy and surprise. The comment was so unlike the taciturn Ethan she'd come to know. She liked this side of him, too. In fact, she liked pretty much everything about him and she couldn't wait to show him just how much.

"What about you?" he asked. "Did you have a good time?"

She cocked her head a little, considering his question carefully. "It was good to see you get the recognition you deserve. There were a lot of envious people in the room there tonight. I'd say you could pick your price if you ever wanted to work for another winery pretty much anywhere in the world."

"I wouldn't do that. I'd never leave The Masters."

His answer was straight to the point, like him. She hadn't realized it until he'd said it that she'd been subconsciously asking a question of him—wondering if he'd ever be willing to set off somewhere new, start fresh without the weight of ties and family obligations. He'd given her the answer she expected. It still gave her a pang of regret. No matter the attraction between them, no matter her new-found feelings for Ethan, she was not the woman for him. He needed someone as committed to The Masters as he was himself. Perhaps even more so, as that woman would need to be committed wholly to him also to fully understand why it was so important for him to continue the traditions of generations of Masterses on South Australian soil.

Isobel was not that person, and acknowledging that blunt truth set up an ache deep inside that she knew would take a long time to ignore. Being busy with her work would be a most excellent way to hurry the process, but in the meantime, she at least had tonight, and maybe another week as she finalized things with Tamsyn and the marketing team over the publicity shots.

When they returned to the apartment, Isobel found herself wanting to prolong every moment with Ethan, to tuck away memories to take out and savor another day. When he suggested a nightcap, she agreed, and they sat in the massive lounge room, overlooking the lights that sparkled in the distance while sipping an aged tawny port.

She kicked off her shoes and pulled her feet up onto the sofa where they sat. When Ethan reached for one foot and began to absently massage it she all but melted under his touch. He turned every part of her body into an erogenous zone. She could only hope she could do the same for him.

And later, in the bedroom, she did her very best so that when they collapsed, exhausted, on their tangled sheets, she felt certain that he'd be as unlikely to forget her as she would to ever, ever forget him.

The persistent buzz of his cell phone vibrating dragged Ethan from a deeply satisfying sleep. He reached for the bedside cabinet and grabbed the phone, sliding from the bed even as he answered it and heading out of the bedroom so he wouldn't disturb Isobel.

"Ethan, it's Rob."

Rob, one of the winemakers who formed an integral part of his team at The Masters, spoke before Ethan could even identify himself. His stomach dropped as he registered the concern in his colleague's voice.

"What is it?" he demanded, knowing Rob wouldn't be calling him this early in the morning unless there was a serious problem.

"It's not good."

Ethan's brows drew together as he listened. Somehow, someone had put the reserve chardonnay in the wrong tank, inadvertently blending it with a lesser quality wine. By the time he ended the call, Ethan felt sick to his stomach. This was a monumental error that should never have happened. He should have been there—he should have stayed at home and remained focused on his work. He shouldn't have gone to the awards ceremony. He hadn't needed the accolade to know what he did was good—he knew what he did was good because he paid attention, because he obsessively kept an eye on progress, because he remained in control.

But he'd relinquished control and look what had happened. Oh, sure, they'd make a good wine in the long run with careful blending and fining. But it wouldn't be produced under the renowned The Masters reserve label—the label he personally undertook to ensure was consistently world class.

"Ethan?" Isobel's voice came from behind him. "Is everything okay?"

He felt every muscle in his body weaken at the sound of her voice. And therein lay the chink in his armor. His weakness.

Isobel.

He turned to face her. Her cheek had a slight mark on it from where she'd lain on the sheets, and her hair was rumpled, her eyes still heavy lidded with sleep. It didn't matter how she looked, how she dressed—or undressed, for that matter—she tempted him every single time. And it had to stop. It had to end, here and now. Tamsyn was wrong. It wasn't worth it to live in the moment—no matter how good the moment might be—if it put everything else at risk.

"No, everything's not okay. There's been a mistake at the winery, one that wouldn't have happened if I had stayed where I should have been all along."

"Oh, no," she cried sympathetically. "Can it be rectified?"

He shrugged. "We'll have to wait and see. The wine itself won't be of the standard or quality it was designated to be. The waste is epic."

Frustration and anger with himself pulled his thoughts

this way and that. A growing cycle wasted. He could only imagine what Raif would say when he heard the news. Raif had built his home within sight of the small vineyard that had escaped the bush fires that had nearly destroyed their family's livelihood so many years ago. He had taken over the nurturing and care of the old vines, and was as vigilant over and proud of his grapes as Ethan was about what he did with their fruit. His cousin would be equally devastated at the news.

"What happened?" Isobel asked, breaking into his thoughts.

"What should never have happened. Two wines were mixed that shouldn't have been, and it's my fault."

"Ethan, you weren't there. You can't blame yourself."

Isobel put a hand on his arm but he shook it off.

"Can't I?" he asked, futile rage beginning to build inside him. "I *should* have been there."

"You have to be able to delegate sometimes, surely."

"And if this is what I can expect when I do?" His mind raced with thoughts of things he should have done, checks he should have put into place to keep something like this from occurring. "The final responsibility rests with me. I am the family head, not anyone else."

"Ethan—"

"No, Isobel. Nothing you say changes anything. When my father died, I took over his obligations. All of them."

"But you had to be here last night," she persisted. "You owed it to yourself, to this brand you speak of and to your family to front up for the award."

"Owed it to myself?" He shook his head slowly. "I didn't come because I wanted to receive the award in person. I could have sent anyone else from The Masters. They could have damn well posted the thing to me in the mail! No, I came because I wanted to be with you. I don't focus when I'm with you.

"I can't trust myself when I'm with you, Isobel. I can't trust myself to be who I'm meant to be—who I was brought up to become. Until I met you nothing and no one could distract me from my work. I believed…I believed I could have both, at least for a little while. I knew you'd be leaving soon, but I thought that while we were here, that we could…that I could… But I can't, don't you see? I can't have you in my life and be good at what I do at the same time. My work has to come first. I owe that to my family, to my father. My work is what will *last*—" *after you go away,* he continued silently in his thoughts.

"And that's why I can't see you anymore."

Isobel staggered back in shock, her face ashen. But he didn't hold back. He couldn't. He took a deep breath.

"I don't want you to come back to The Masters with me. You can stay here as long as you need to. I'll get the building concierge to key your fingerprint into the biometric reader. You can communicate with Tamsyn via the phone and the internet, but I think it's better if we end this here and now. You've finished the job you came here to do. Dragging it out won't do either one of us any good."

"Do you really think sending me off will make things better? Hiding from your feelings won't make them go away. You have to be stronger than that."

"What? Like my father was strong? Like my mother leaving him didn't change him? He could have gone after her, you know. But he chose to stay—to focus on his family, to focus on the winery. It's what I have to do, too." He held up a hand as she started to protest. "No, please. Hear me out on this, Isobel. This thing we have together, it consumes me. I lose control when I'm with you—my temper, my passion, my joy. Everything. I can't allow myself to be that man.

"I'm going to get dressed and head home. I'll leave it to you as to what you do next, but please, don't come back to the winery."

"Ethan, please, think about this some more before you go. I know you're upset. I know what's happened with the wine is a big deal, but it's happened. Can't you just let it go? Move on?"

He ignored the wobble in her voice and reached deep for what he had to say next.

"I am moving on, Isobel. We're too different to make a relationship between us work. One of us will always end up hurt as a result. It's what happened to my parents, and I won't have it happen to me, too. My mother was…like you. A free spirit. And when she couldn't take being tied down anymore, she decided to leave my father. Take Tamsyn and me and leave him. Pull us from our birthright and our father. No wonder he paid her to stay away after that."

He rubbed his eyes with one hand and fought to push back the overwhelming sense of bleakness that now threatened to swamp him. "You and I, we have no future together. You go wherever the wind takes you, but I stay here. 'Here' is all I've got. And I can't let my feelings for you distract me from that. Which is why I can't have you around."

Isobel stared at him in disbelief. She swallowed against the emotion burning in her throat, determined she wouldn't show him for even so much as one second how much his words just now had hurt her.

"Fine. I won't return to The Masters. I'm just about finished up, anyway. I can complete any last-minute things via email with Tamsyn."

To her surprise her voice was steady and sure, as sure as her determination to refuse to show Ethan just how deep his words had cut her and how much she'd found herself wishing he'd asked her to stay.

Thank God she hadn't told him that she loved him. That would be the ultimate irony, the ultimate weakness. She, who'd never wanted to stay or settle with any one person, and especially not to fall in love, was head over heels with a man who, it appeared, was willing to toss her aside, anyway.

"Thank you for not making this awkward," he said, his voice devoid of expression.

She looked at him, struggled to believe this was the same man who'd laughed with her last night, who'd loved with her in the darkness. The man who'd stolen her heart.

Her lips twisted in an ironic smile. "I'll go now. Just give me a few minutes to get my things together. Good luck with your work. I really do hope you'll be happy. You deserve to be happy, Ethan. Remember that."

Somehow she found the strength to turn away from him without touching him, to make her way to the bathroom where she showered quickly and dressed in her standard uniform of jeans and a shirt then, without checking to see if he was still in the main living area waiting for her, she hefted her pack onto her shoulders and let herself out the second entrance they'd used last night.

She had her pack, and her health and a sizeable check on its way to fatten her bank account soon. Those were all the things she'd ever needed to get by. They were all she'd need now. They'd have to be…because the chance of having anything else was now over.

Fifteen

Isobel was at the airport waiting for her flight to Singapore. From there she was heading back to Africa and it couldn't be soon enough, she decided. Her cell phone began to vibrate in her pocket and she slid it out to check the caller ID. Tamsyn. She sighed. Every instinct told her to ignore the call, to keep things purely to email between them. Too much could be read into tone of voice and she didn't want anyone to know what an idiot she'd been to fall in love with Ethan Masters, especially not his sister.

But Tamsyn had been her friend, as well. She owed it to her to speak to her directly. Isobel thumbed the pad of her phone, answering the call.

"Isobel? Are you okay?"

"I'm fine, Tamsyn. Just got a heads-up on my next project and I needed to take advantage of it. I'm sorry not to have been able to say goodbye in person."

"Really? Is that why you're leaving so soon? Ethan came

back here like a bear with a sore head. I know he's upset about the reserve but I thought... Well, never mind what I thought. I'm sorry, too."

Silence stretched out between them for a moment or two. Isobel forced herself to speak.

"Look, they'll be calling my flight soon. I have to go. Thanks for everything, Tam, and you take care, okay? I'll email you."

"Yeah, sure. Look, I wanted to let you know that I've decided to try and find my mother, to at least find out where she is."

"Are you sure that's wise? You might end up opening a whole can of worms you're not ready for."

"I know," Tamsyn agreed. "That's why I'm not rushing into anything. It's not as if I don't have enough other stuff to keep me busy, anyway. But I need to know more about her."

"I understand, but be very careful about what you decide to do once you do have the information you're looking for. Promise me? Things may not always turn out the way you hope they will."

Tamsyn gave a short, dry laugh. "Is that the voice of experience talking now, Isobel?"

Isobel closed her eyes for a moment, shutting out the busyness of the terminal building and focusing on her friend's voice, on imagining her in her office, overlooking the property and the people who worked there.

"Yeah, maybe," she admitted.

"You can always come back, Isobel."

"No, I can't," she said softly. "I never look back."

"Are you sure you can't make an exception this time?"

"No exceptions, Tam. I'm sorry. Look, it's been wonderful getting to know you. I meant it about staying in touch, okay? And let me know how things are going with your search for your mother."

"Sure, I will. Take care, Isobel. I'll miss you."

"I'll miss you, too."

Isobel disconnected the call, not wanting to actually say goodbye, not wanting to hear it in return. Because that would make her leaving all the more final.

Ethan looked at Shanal across the intimate dining table at the select restaurant he'd chosen to bring her to tonight. The past couple of weeks had been difficult. Coming to grips with the accident at the winery was one thing; getting used to the fact that Isobel was no longer nearby was something else entirely. He gave himself a mental shake. Dwelling on the past was not going to consolidate his future, a future he hoped would include the woman seated across from him.

Shanal's pale green eyes glittered in the soft lighting in the dining room. Her long, black hair was a glossy fall down her back. She was beautiful, intelligent, warm and friendly. Everything he wanted in a life mate—especially when he factored in her steady and reliable nature.

The waiter brought their coffee and withdrew, reminding Ethan that the evening was drawing to a close and he had yet to broach the subject of marriage with Shanal. He drew in a deep breath and let it out slowly before reaching across the small table to take Shanal's hand.

She looked up at him, startled by his action.

"Shanal, do you often think about the future?"

She gave him a nervous smile. "The future? Of course I do. All the time, actually."

"So do I," Ethan said with more confidence. "And I think we make a good pair, don't you?"

"Ethan, I—"

He rushed on, interrupting her. "We should get married. We're great friends already. We have the same interests, the same wants. We would be great together."

To his absolute shock, Shanal burst out laughing.

"What?" he asked, more than a bit put out by her reaction.

"Oh, Ethan. Surely you're not serious?"

He thought for a moment of the ring set with diamonds and an unusual pale green amethyst he had stowed in his pocket. One he'd chosen for its uniqueness and because it reminded him of the exact color of Shanal's eyes. "Why wouldn't I be serious about it?"

"Because you're in love with someone else. Besides, I'm not *in* love with you and, call me old-fashioned, but I think love is definitely a prerequisite for a long and happy marriage, don't you?"

"But I do love you," he protested, even as his gut clenched.

"Sure, and I love you, too, but not *that* way." She tugged her hand free. "Ethan, we're great friends and I hope we'll always share that special relationship no matter where we are or what we're doing. When you started asking me out, I was willing to try to see if there could be something more between us. I thought you'd realized, as I did, that there couldn't—and that that was why I hadn't heard from you for the past few weeks. When you rang to ask me out tonight, I was expecting you to admit the truth—that we're better off as friends."

"Are we?"

"Of course we are. It's not just that you're not in love with me. It's that you *are* in love with Isobel. Even a blind man could see that. You're crazy not to grasp what the two of you could have and hold tight. You owe it to yourself, and to her, to keep it safe forever because a love like that doesn't come along in every lifetime."

"Isobel?"

Shanal huffed a sigh of frustration. "You know, for an intelligent man, you can be hopelessly dense sometimes. Yes, Isobel. Tell me, how did you feel the first time you ever saw her?"

"Like I'd suddenly found light in a dark place."

She smiled. "Exactly. And what did you do?"

"I followed her."

"And then?" she prompted.

Ethan felt heat rise into his cheeks. He wasn't about to share with Shanal what had happened next. She obviously noted the high color in his face.

"See what I mean? When has anyone ever made you feel like she did, behave like you did together? It was way more than infatuation or lust, Ethan. Don't forget, I know you well. I knew you had some crazy bee in your bonnet about us, but when I saw you with Isobel I wondered if you weren't fighting against her just a little too hard."

She lifted her coffee cup and took a sip and eyed him over the china rim. "Seriously, what are you afraid of? You have the chance to have the kind of forever love that many people can only dream of. I envy you that because that's the kind of love I want from the man I marry, if I ever marry. And you can be certain I'm not prepared to settle for less than that, ever."

"Are you sure, Shanal? We could be a great partnership." He had to try, just one more time, because what she was suggesting was impossible and scary all at the same time.

"I'm one hundred percent certain. Now, enjoy your coffee and take me home and we can put this behind us and get back to normal again."

By the time he arrived home and went upstairs to his room, he felt shattered. Building up to tonight had taken more out of him than he'd expected and, oddly, he now even felt some relief that Shanal had turned him down. It seemed she knew him better than he knew himself, he thought with a rueful smile as he unknotted his tie and threw it at an easy chair in the corner of his room.

His attention was dragged to the open drapes at his window, to the darkness beyond that served as a reminder of the empty cottage where Isobel had stayed. Where they'd made love. A fist clenched tight in his gut. He'd sent her away and she'd gone, willingly. On to the next thing, the next adventure, the next job, the next man.

The thought made him feel physically ill and he snapped his drapes closed with a decisive flick. Shanal could say what she liked about him and Isobel having a special connection. The truth was, she'd had one foot out the door from the moment she arrived at The Masters. Sending her away had shortened her stay, but nothing he could have done would have made her stay for good.

A knock at his door made him turn around.

"It's only me," Tamsyn said through the door. "Can I come in?"

"Sure," he said, pulling the door open. "What's up?"

"I just wanted to see if congratulations were in order."

"Me and Shanal? No. She turned me down."

"Oh, thank God!"

Ethan looked at his sister in shock. "You think we would have been such a bad match?"

"No, not that, but you wouldn't have been happy. Not really happy like you deserve."

Her words echoed the ones Isobel had parted from him with. "I'll never know now, will I?" he said flippantly.

"You will if you do something about Isobel."

"Like what?"

"Like tell her how you really feel."

It seemed everyone knew him better than he knew himself. Strangely, the thought didn't rankle as he thought it might.

"What's the point? My life is here, and she'd never want to settle down."

"You could try asking her, you know."

"Asking her to give up her whole life? Her work? Her plans?"

"Ask her if she'd be willing to try. There's a chance you could reach a compromise, if you're willing to work for one. I've never known you to turn away from something just because it would be hard work. Usually you take that sort of thing as a challenge. What do you have to lose by asking?"

"And what if I'm afraid to? Have you ever considered that?"

"You, Ethan? Afraid?" Tamsyn looked stunned, as if the idea had never occurred to her. She pressed her lips together, her expression showing she was thinking hard. "Okay, I get that you'd be careful—you're not the sort to rush into anything—but afraid? Why?"

Ethan sat down on one of the easy chairs positioned in front of the stone fireplace in his room and motioned for his sister to do the same. "We haven't exactly had the best examples set for us, have we? Aunt Cynthia and Uncle Charles split up and put their kids through hell. Dad let us think that Mum was dead all this time—and she was so eager to get away from him that she did nothing to show us otherwise. Even Uncle Edward and Aunt Marianne haven't always been smooth sailing."

"No, but that doesn't mean we can't make a success of things ourselves. If all people ever looked at through history was failure, without changing something to do it better, then humankind would cease to exist."

He smiled at her words. She was right. But that was what he'd done already—tried to improve on the past, to fix mistakes and avoid the same pitfalls.

"I have done it differently than Mum and Dad. I've been careful. I haven't led with my heart."

"Sure, but at the cost of all else," Tamsyn protested. "You try to wrap everything around you in cotton wool. You don't take risks, you only bet on a sure thing and you're so protective of me and the family it's almost suffocating."

Suffocating? Is that what she thought? A flare of frustration warred with sadness that she felt that way. He felt obligated to respond.

"When Mum died, or at least when we were led to believe she had, I felt as if the cornerstone of my world had crumbled away. Dad was always so busy here that she was our real compass. You're probably too young to remember the way she was with us. One time, I remember she was dressed up for a ladies' tea somewhere. But when she heard we were off to the creek with some of the other cousins, she kicked off her high heels, threw on a pair of flip-flops and came with us. Just like that. She was always there for us and then all of a sudden she wasn't.

"In the hospital, after the accident, Dad told me to be his little man, to look after you, and I did. Maybe I took that a little too far."

"Don't be too hard on yourself," Tamsyn said softly. "You're a great big brother and I know how lucky I've been. But I am a grown-up now. Don't take this the wrong way, but when I need your help, I will ask for it. You don't need to make my decisions for me anymore."

Ethan accepted the truth of her words, even though a

part of him still struggled to let go. It was going to take some rethinking on his part, but he'd get there. Looking out for his family was firmly entrenched in him, but he'd try to be less smothering, more accepting of everyone's right to make their own decisions. And that began right now with Tamsyn and their mother.

"You want to find her, don't you?"

"I need to," she answered simply.

He sighed softly. "Then I'll do whatever I can to help you."

"Thank you. And I'll do whatever I can to help you, too."

He smiled at her earnestness. Deep down she was still his baby sister, still seeking his approval, still eager to please.

"Help me?" he asked, not entirely sure what she was angling at.

"With Isobel. With getting her back." He started to protest, but she held up a hand to cut him off. "If you're going to let me make my own decisions, then you definitely have to let Isobel make hers, as well. At least tell her how you feel. Then let her take it from there."

"I don't even know where to begin," he answered in all honesty. "Our chemistry aside, I hardly know anything about her except she's good at what she does and she travels a lot."

"Start with her blog, 'IF Only.' You'll understand what's important to her. The rest will come." Tamsyn rose from her chair and bent to kiss Ethan on the cheek. "You'll do what's right. You always do. G'night."

He raised a hand in acknowledgment as she left the room and closed the door behind her. He was alone with his thoughts. Thoughts he hadn't wanted to believe or acknowledge. But he couldn't ignore them now. He'd been trying so hard to do the right thing, to be the right man, and in doing so he'd probably lost the best thing that had ever happened to him in his entire life.

He didn't know if he could convince her to give a relationship between them a chance, but he had to try. Somehow, he had to get Isobel back.

Sixteen

Ethan's eyes burned the next morning. He'd been up until the small hours reading Isobel's blog and experiencing a welling sense of shame in the way he'd treated her. He'd thought her careless, bohemian, incapable of commitment—yet she was so much more than any of those things. She was always on the go, without any of the attachments he cherished, but she used her freedom to help people, and make a difference in so many lives.

His conscience still stung with embarrassment when he thought about the throwaway comment he'd made to her one day about taking mall photos of grumpy babies and toddlers. The photos she'd put up on the internet, the devastation and poverty, the homeless children and uprooted families—they were so powerful and moving. She'd walked in the shadow of those people, some still proud and fighting for what they believed in, others beaten and bowed. Yet every person she'd featured had been treated with a dignity and respect he hadn't even had the grace to afford Isobel herself.

They said the bigger you were the harder the fall. Well, he'd fallen—hard. His arrogance and presumption left a bitter echo in his mind, one he was determined to rinse out and to never, ever allow back into his thinking again.

While the photos Isobel had taken were shocking and carried a powerful message—sometimes of hope, other times of despair—it was her commentary that showed how clever and insightful she was and how deeply she respected her subjects. It was easy to see how committed she was to highlighting their plight and the need to effect change in their world.

He particularly admired the series she'd done just before coming to Australia—one that had focused on the infants and small children struggling to survive in a refugee camp on the border of two war-torn countries. And here he was, still fuming about the loss of a tank of wine. He had been such a fool. Guilt riddled his conscience. Had he bothered, even just once, to try and truly understand what mattered to Isobel? He knew she loved her work, but he'd never made even a fraction of the effort to understand her commitment to photography that she'd made to understand his passion for wine. He only hoped that he could have another chance to put things right between them.

After he finished work that day, Ethan checked her blog again, rereading some of the entries Isobel had made before she'd come to The Masters. In them he noticed an undercurrent of concern that she might not be able to complete the task she'd set herself. One entry finished with a brief comment stating she'd been cordially invited to leave the country and to avoid any further confrontations. She'd done exactly that. The way she'd worded it, he could almost hear her breezy tone downplaying the seriousness of the event. Reading between the lines, however, it sounded as if she'd narrowly avoided imprisonment for her activities.

Ethan scrolled through the blog until he reached her most recent entry. In it she talked about the hiatus she'd enjoyed in South Australia and she'd used a picture she'd obviously taken while exploring the ruins up on the hill. She'd then expanded a little on returning to the refugee camps to complete what she'd started earlier. Her commentary sent him on a web search and what he found made his blood run cold. No matter how lightly she worded it, Isobel was investigating illegal border crossings and the people who facilitated them. What she was doing was a clear breach of media regulations.

A sick feeling of dread swept through him as he considered the circumstances surrounding her departure from the warring nation the last time she'd visited, and the likelihood of her coming to harm if she ever returned. He checked the date of her most recent blog entry. Just over two weeks ago. Nothing since. It wasn't like her. Given the example of her many previous trips away, she usually posted at least once, sometimes twice a week. Maybe he'd missed something. He refreshed the page. Nothing.

He opened another window on his computer, his fingers rapping against the keys until he found what he was searching for. Bile rose in his throat as he read the news report stating a female international photographer had been detained by military forces on behalf of the government on a charge of media infringement. The dates matched. The location matched. It had to be Isobel.

Isobel squatted on her haunches, her back against the filthy wall behind her. She was equally filthy, her skin crawling, her hair matted and dull, her stomach an aching pit alternately craving food then griping painfully over the weevil-filled slop she and the other prisoners were spo-radically given. She'd begun to lose track of time and she knew that was a bad thing. Without the progression of days and nights, weeks, this entire nightmare would fade into a blur and she was afraid she'd disappear into the over-crowded numbers of people being detained on a variety of charges—some valid, many not so valid.

A commotion at the entrance to the cell she shared with twenty-seven other women failed to even attract her attention until she felt hands pulling at her, dragging her forward.

"They want you, miss," one of her cell mates hissed at her under her breath. "Go, now, before they come in and get you."

Isobel staggered to her feet, her breath catching as her circulation restored and painful pins and needles flooded her lower limbs.

"Isobel Fyfe?" a uniformed guard barked at her with narrowed eyes.

She nodded. "Yes, that's me."

"This way."

The cell door clanged closed behind her as she followed the guard down the narrow cell-lined corridor. Shouts and cries from other prisoners followed her.

"What's happening? Why have you called me?" she asked, but the guard continued to walk ahead, eventually slowing to open a door.

When she didn't enter immediately, he grabbed her shoulder and pushed her through, shutting and locking the door behind her—exchanging one form of imprison-ment for another. She wheeled around, banging her hands on the solid wood, shouting for an explanation, but none was forthcoming. It could have been ten minutes later, it could have been an hour, but eventually the door reopened to reveal an older man in a suit, his skin so pale it was obvious he was not a resident here.

"Miss Fyfe, I'm glad we found you. Let me introduce myself. Colin James. I'm with the New Zealand Embassy. We've secured your release."

"My release?" She barely believed her ears. "But how did you know I was here?"

"Let's just say you have friends with influence. Besides, the important thing is you're being discharged, so let's not go into the legalities, shall we? I think we'd be best advised to make haste before they change their minds."

She didn't argue, but one thing still worried her. "The man who was with me, is he—"

The look on Mr. James's face told her everything. "I'm sorry m'dear."

A swell of grief threatened to overwhelm her, but she fought it back. There'd be time to give in to her sorrow when she was away from here. Away and safe. She was so lucky that she had someone, somewhere, who could advocate for her. Her guide had not been so fortunate and he'd paid the ultimate price. She'd find some way to get money to his family and she'd try, somehow, to get them away from here. It was the very least she could do. She swallowed against the lump in her throat before getting her thoughts back in order.

"My things, my cameras?"

"Forfeit, I'm afraid."

"Everything? Even my clothing?"

"I understand your pack was confiscated along with everything inside and whatever you had in your possession at the time of your arrest. We have negotiated the return of your passport on condition you understand that should you ever set foot here again, you will be arrested on sight. You have been classified an enemy of the current regime and I cannot advise you strongly enough that it is in your best interests that once you're out of here, you stay away."

She nodded. Three weeks in prison had been an eye-opening experience. She'd always imagined that, should the situation arise, she'd be prepared for anything. But she couldn't have been more wrong. She was as committed to her work as ever, but now that she was intimately acquainted with the consequences, she could never be as blasé about the risks as she'd been in the past. Maybe the time had come to learn to be more careful, more meticulous in her planning, more cautious in choosing her targets. If she'd been less reckless, she might have been able to avoid imprisonment altogether. It was an experience she never wanted to repeat.

The only thing that had kept her sane had been thinking about The Masters. About the long, rolling lines of grapevines, about the silhouetted ruin on the hill reminding everyone that even in adversity, life could begin anew. About Ethan. Again, tears burned in the back of her throat and she fought to control the trembling that shook her body.

"I understand. We should go then. Thank you."

Her things she could replace and although the memory cards and her recent photos were a loss, they were nothing compared to the forfeit of a human life. She had been so lucky to be travelling on a New Zealand passport. She was so relieved that, even though she hadn't set foot in the country of her birth since she and her father had left ten years ago, she still had the benefit of a government division that had fought for her release.

It wasn't until she was in Johannesburg, awaiting her flight to Singapore, that she finally began to feel safe again—although even once she was airborne, she couldn't relax enough to sleep. She was foggy with exhaustion as she transited in Singapore, checking into an airport hotel for one night before catching a flight to Auckland, New Zealand. It was time to go home. Time to reassess her life, her priorities.

She still felt sick to her soul that she'd been responsible for the death of her guide. Logically, she knew that it hadn't been her who had pulled the trigger on the man, but he had been in the wrong place at the wrong time because of her. She'd have to institute some new precautions during her assignments going forward—not just for her sake, but for the sake of those with her.

Isobel took out a short-term lease on a furnished inner-city apartment on her arrival in Auckland, and spent the next month recovering her strength. She still woke screaming in the night, clawing at the monsters that weren't there and filled with the terror of her arrest and subsequent incarceration. Some days she was fine, ready to pick up her new cameras and to start all over again. Other days, she did nothing more than ride back and forth on the ferry between Devonport and Auckland city center, lost in her thoughts and the changing faces and accents that surrounded her.

She was grieving, she rationalized on her better days. For her guide, for the people whose lives she'd failed to make a positive difference in, for herself and the life she'd so guilelessly accepted as her right, for the love she'd borne for a man who couldn't possibly ever love her in return, and for the mother she'd never had a proper chance to say goodbye to.

She'd spent so much of her life running, avoiding attachment by staying on the go. It wasn't until she'd been literally unable to move, locked up in a jail cell that she was forced to truly examine her life. She wasn't happy with all that she'd found. It was time to stop running from herself—to accept her past, and come to terms with what she wanted for her future.

She'd been home about six weeks before she finally discovered exactly where her mother had been buried. She rode a series of buses out to the graveyard on the outskirts of the sprawling city. The weathered, small, wooden cross was little reminder of all that her mother had been and all they'd left behind when Isobel and her father had left New Zealand. She sank to her knees beside the marker. Her mother had deserved more than this. Her memory deserved more than this. Running away from the reality of his wife's death might have been her father's way of dealing with things, but it hadn't been fair to the woman who'd loved him to leave her behind without a suitable memorial to mark her passing.

Isobel lost track of time there, kneeling in the grass alone with her thoughts and memories. She was stiff and cold when she finally rose and left the graveyard. But even though she'd grown uncomfortable physically, she felt more at peace than she had in a very long time. Later, back at her apartment, she opened her new laptop and searched for monumental masons. Now she was home it was time to do right by her mother and really put her to rest. That started with a suitably inscribed headstone. One with her mother's favorite line of poetry forever linked with her name.

While on her laptop, Isobel checked the online storage cache of her work. Despite patchy internet connections, she'd managed to upload most of her pictures except the shots she'd taken on the day she was arrested. Her hand trembled as it hovered over the mouse pad and she had to dig deep for the courage to open the album, to look again into the eyes of the man who'd given his life in her service and in the service of his people.

She scrolled through the album, tears running unchecked down her cheeks, her stomach tied in knots. When she was done, she signed in to her blog and wrote and wrote and wrote some more, until her heart ached a little less and her eyes burned, dry now and scratchy and sore.

Then, finally, she slept.

Isobel was pushing breakfast around her plate at a small café the next day when she checked her blog. A small cry of amazement passed her lips when she saw the outpouring of support for her post, support with offers both financial and physical to help wherever and however people could. And there, buried amongst them all, was a comment from Tamsyn, together with a request for Isobel to message her privately.

She leaned back in her chair, and debated whether she should just let that part of her life go, put it behind her. Never look back, she reminded herself. It had been her modus operandi for so long, it went against everything she'd schooled herself to be to get in touch with Tamsyn now. After all she'd been through, the life her friend led seemed ever more distant than it had before. Maybe it was time to make a clean break after all.

Coward, her conscience chided her. Self-preservation, she silently argued back. She had no desire to hear about Ethan's marriage plans with Shanal, and if she contacted Tamsyn she had no doubt her friend would feel obliged to bring her up-to-date. It plagued her the rest of the day, until she caught sight of a society column in an online paper. Tamsyn's name was mentioned. Apparently, she was visiting with her cousin and his wife in Auckland.

Before Isobel could overthink things, she fired an email off to her friend and, to her surprise, a reply lobbed straight back in, suggesting they meet for lunch the next day. Isobel was shocked to realize that this would be her first social interaction with another human being since she'd left

Africa. She'd become so introspective, so reclusive, since her imprisonment and release. It was time to rectify that.

Seeing Tamsyn in the hotel lobby where they'd agreed to meet, Isobel was hard-pressed not to fly across the polished tile floors and launch herself into her friend's arms. She hadn't allowed herself to realize just how much she'd missed Tamsyn until now, when they stood here face-to-face.

"Oh, my God, Isobel, you've lost so much weight. Are you okay?" The words tumbled from Tamsyn's lips as she reached for Isobel and hugged her tight. "You're all skin and bone. C'mon, let's hit the restaurant. You definitely need feeding up. My treat."

Once they were seated, Tamsyn leaned forward and reached for Isobel's hand.

"Tell me," she urged. "Are you okay? Really okay? I read your blog post. It must have been wretched."

Isobel gave her a weak smile. "That's one word for it, yeah."

"I'm so relieved you're safely home. So, tell me what you've been doing since you've been back."

Isobel shrugged. "Nothing. I've sorted out a headstone for my mother's grave and that's about it. I can't seem to get motivated to work or to do anything about showing any of my work. I just feel so directionless."

"You've been through a lot," Tamsyn sympathized. "You'll come right with time."

"But will I? Most days I don't even feel like picking up a camera again. Photography has been my life for so long, I'm terrified at the thought that I'm never going to be able to do it again. I really believed coming back to New Zealand would help, that it would make me feel as if I'd come full circle, ready to start the next stage of my life. But it's all I can do to even get out of bed each day."

Tamsyn picked up a teaspoon and absently stirred her coffee, the look of concern on her face almost Isobel's undoing. She'd managed to stay strong for a couple of days now but faced with her friend's worry on her behalf, she felt the all-too-familiar tears rise near the surface again.

"Listen to me. I haven't even asked how you're doing," Isobel said, struggling to pull herself together.

"I'm fine, but I'm worried about you, Isobel. You don't look or sound like yourself. I know you've been through a harrowing experience, and that it takes time to recover from something like that, if you even can fully recover from what you went through. But the Isobel I know wouldn't let anything or anyone strip the light out of her life."

"You're right. I've let them win," Isobel said bleakly. "I need to fight back."

"Or maybe you need to take a few steps back. Regroup, regain your strength. Have you thought about why you're having so much trouble?"

"Not really," she admitted helplessly.

"Maybe you should. And maybe you should think about whether part of this languor you're suffering from isn't because you're missing Ethan."

That really made her sit up straight. "Ethan? Why would I be fretting over him? He was the one who told me to leave. I was too much of a distraction, apparently. And I was keeping him from his work."

Tamsyn laughed. "Is that what he told you? Seriously? Did you never stop to consider that maybe he was scared? Scared to love you? You're so different yet so perfect for one another. The perfect complement."

"Not as perfect as Shanal, apparently. How are their

wedding plans coming along?" Try as she might, Isobel couldn't quite keep a touch of snark out of her tone.

"They're not. He isn't marrying Shanal. They're great friends but totally unsuited for anything else, and they know it. You know, you should think really hard about where you go next, Isobel. Look deep inside and follow your heart."

"I've always followed my heart. It's what I've made my reputation doing."

Tamsyn waved aside her words as if they were of no consequence. "I'm not talking about causes. There's a difference between following a cause that's close to your heart and true love. Think about it, Isobel. True love can move mountains…and governments."

Isobel jolted at Tamsyn's last words. Governments? Was Tamsyn suggesting what she thought she was suggesting? The New Zealand embassy representative *had* mentioned she had friends with influence, and she'd struggled to think who they could have been. The only way to find out was to ask outright, but her mouth struggled to form the words. Eventually, though, she managed to speak.

"Was Ethan behind my release?"

"Look, he made me swear not to tell a soul what he did but since you've put two and two together, I'm not going to lie to you."

Tamsyn went on to give Isobel the full story about how Ethan had pulled every last favor he'd been owed, contacted every friend in high places in Australia and New Zealand, as well as every government contact he'd ever made, and hounded them to pull the necessary strings to see to it that Isobel was released.

Isobel didn't know what to think, what to feel. It was an emotional slap upside the head that she hadn't been expecting.

"He loves you, Isobel, and I know you love him, too. He can be overbearing, but it's all right sometimes, isn't it? It's how he found you, and got you home safe. I know wanderlust is your middle name but can't you find some way to make it work between you? From what I can tell, you're both miserable apart."

"We weren't all that happy together. We were too busy fighting." Isobel attempted to reason but was rewarded with a look of irritation from Tamsyn that made her firmly shut her mouth.

"If you weren't happy it's because you were both fighting what, deep down inside, you both wanted all along. For goodness' sake, Isobel—don't you want to be happy?"

"Of course I do, and I am…mostly."

Tamsyn groaned aloud, earning them a strange look from the couple at the table next to them.

"I swear, Isobel, the pair of you are enough to wear out the patience of a saint. Seriously. Look, don't make any decisions here and now. Think about what I've said and ask yourself, deep down, what's most important. I've done my part."

"Thank you," Isobel said, reaching to squeeze her friend's hand. "I don't deserve you."

"Of course you do, and more. So grab it, Isobel. You came close to losing your life without ever really living it. Don't you owe it to yourself to at least try?"

About to argue that she'd lived her life more fully than most, Isobel hesitated. She knew what Tamsyn was talking about. For all she'd done, for all her travels, she'd never risked her heart. She'd never, not once, taken that leap of faith and put her happiness in the hands of another person. But could she? Could she trust another person so much, so deeply, and put her carefully constructed world at the mercy of another?

There was only one way to find out.

Seventeen

Ethan looked out his office window as the shiny red hatchback pulled up outside the winery. He didn't recognize the car and, to his knowledge, they weren't expecting anyone today. His heart skidded across a few beats when he recognized the slender blond-haired woman who got out from the driver's side.

Isobel? What on earth...?

Before he realized it, he was out of his chair and headed outside. He had to be mistaken, surely. But no, the woman standing opposite him was indeed Isobel, albeit a pale, hollowed-out version of the bright butterfly he remembered. Every male protective instinct welled to instant life inside of him and he fought the urge to sweep her up in his arms and make everything better in her world once more.

His eyes raked over her, taking in the fact she'd lost weight, noting the lack of health in her skin and the missing gleam in her hair. She was a shell of who she used to be, but at least she was still alive, he reassured himself. He had that to take pleasure in at the very least. And she was here.

"Is it true?" she said abruptly, her voice a rasp on the chill winter air. "Are you responsible for my freedom?"

It was a loaded question, one with multiple answers if you examined the various layers of what freedom was. Ethan opted for the simplest of them all.

"Yes."

"How?"

"I called in some favors," he said, downplaying the many phone calls and emails he'd made and sent once he figured out that Isobel had been arrested.

"They must have been some favors," she commented.

He had no answer for that. How could he tell her that he'd been prepared to move heaven and earth to ensure her safety? He only wished he could have been there himself when she was freed, to shepherd her safely home. But the idea had been impossible. For one thing, he hadn't wanted her to know that he'd been involved. He hadn't wanted her to feel indebted to him. Instead, he'd reminded himself daily of the old saying, "If you love something, set it free. If it was yours, it will come back to you. If it doesn't, it was never meant to be."

He had all but given up hope of seeing her again, but here she was.

"Why, Ethan? Why did you do that for me?" she asked, her hands clenched in tight balls at her sides.

"Look, why don't we go inside the house and talk. It's cold out and I swear your lips are turning bluer by the minute."

She let him take her elbow and guide her to the main house. He was relieved that, aside from the handful of staff he could hear at the back of the house, none of the family was home. He settled Isobel on a sofa in the small sitting room that Tamsyn liked to use when she was home, and added an extra log of wood to the fire. He hadn't been kidding about Isobel turning blue out there. She was so cold, she was shivering.

Ethan sat next to her and, taking her hands, chafed them together between his larger, warmer ones. Finally, the shivering stopped.

"Sorry I'm being such a wimp," she said.

"You're not a wimp. Here, I'll go and organize some tea for us. You stay by the fire until I'm back."

He was gone a bare five minutes but every second felt like forever. When he carried the tray through to the sitting room, he almost expected to discover that she'd been a figment of his imagination all along. But to his relief, she remained on the sofa where he'd seated her. He poured a mug of tea and added the small dash of milk he knew she preferred before handing her the mug.

"Thanks," she said, wrapping her fingers around the ceramic cup and lifting it to her mouth to sip at its contents. "So tell me, Ethan, why did you work so hard for my release?"

"Tamsyn told you, didn't she? I asked her—"

"I made her. I needed to know. It's why I'm here."

Ethan felt his body sag, the tension escaping him as quickly as it had arisen. It wasn't love that had brought her here—just gratitude. "All this way just to say thank you? There was no need. I just want you to be happy and safe, Isobel. Isn't that enough?"

"But why is that so important to you?"

She wasn't going to let go until he told her the full truth. Ethan looked her square in the eye and hoped she'd be strong enough for the truth.

"Because I love you, Isobel Fyfe. I would move mountains for you if it was necessary."

Twin spots of color highlighted her cheeks, but she said nothing. Then, to his shock, her face crumpled, her eyes welled with tears and she began to cry—huge wrenching sobs that racked her body. Ethan took the mug from her hands before she could spill hot tea on her legs, then pulled her into his arms, holding her frail frame against him as if he could absorb her sorrow and make everything better again. He wished it could be so easy. Instead, he just had to wait while she cried it out. And hold her, just hold her, and thank God she was safe.

Eventually, her sobs quieted and she pulled back a little. "I'm sorry," she said, swiping at the moisture on her face. "I haven't been the same since…"

He wasn't surprised. He'd heard little about her ordeal in Africa but reading between the lines of her latest blog entry, it hadn't been pleasant.

"It's okay," he hastened to reassure her. "You're safe now. You're here, with me."

"And you love me?"

Her voice was tiny, as if she hardly dared believe the words she'd just said. He put everything into his response. All the fear, all the worry, all the relief when he'd heard she'd been released.

"I love you with all my heart."

A tremor ran through her and she lifted her tear-stained face, her watery gaze meeting his. "No one has ever loved me like that before."

"You've never let anyone close enough to love you, have you?" Ethan asked with unerring accuracy. "Will you let me into your heart, Isobel? Will you let me love you?"

"I want to."

She was still scared, still wary. Ethan knew what he had to do next.

"It's safe to let go, Isobel. Safe to love me back if that's what you want to do, and I hope you do. But if you don't, that's okay, too. I could live with that, provided I know you're okay and that you're happy. It took a lot for me to realize it, but you're the most important thing in my whole world. I'm here for you, always.

"I know how important your work is to you and I'm embarrassed that I never considered the importance of what you do and how vital it is to you. How good you are at what you do. I understand that now. I know you need to travel and I know you can't be tied down to any one place or any one person but, if you'll only let me, I will support you in whatever you want to do provided that, from time to time, you come back to me."

Isobel heard the words coming from Ethan's lips. Just simple words but filled with so much meaning. They both terrified her and yet gave her hope, healing that place inside of her that had felt empty and barren for so long.

She looked at him with new eyes. He loved her. It was a gift beyond compare. And even though he loved her, he still anticipated nothing from her in return, except perhaps her love. There were no demands, no expectations. With him she'd be as free to do whatever she wanted, be whomever she wanted, as she'd been all her life.

Maybe this was the true meaning of love, after all. This freedom, the give and take. The all-consuming devotion of her parents for one another had excluded her on so many levels and had left her father a damaged and broken man. One who'd remained on the run from his own feelings, his own grief, until his breaking heart had eventually given out on him and taken him at a time of his life when he should still have been in his prime.

Could she believe that with Ethan she could have a true partnership? One with give and take on both sides? He was willing to do so much to be the man she needed him to be. Could she be the woman *he* needed? She wanted the answer to be yes. She had no doubt that he was that man for her. Not a doubt in the world. It was more than she'd ever dreamed of having, this opportunity, this gift. With his love in her life she would have more freedom than she could ever believe possible—the freedom to love unconditionally.

But only if she had the strength to reach out and grab it.

Not so very long ago she'd have run from this chance at happiness—hell, she *had* run rather than stay and fight for it, even after she knew how she felt about him. And look where that had landed her.

She entangled her fingers with Ethan's and dragged his hands to her lips, pressing a kiss to his knuckles.

"Thank you," she said. "Thank you for being you, for loving me, for freeing me."

"Oh, Isobel, you're easy to love."

"But why me? Why now? When I left, you were so adamant we were wrong together."

Ethan sighed and bowed his head for a minute. When he lifted it again he had a look of shame on his face.

"I was wrong. I was scared. It's no excuse, I know. I couldn't handle the weight of my own feelings for you so I pushed you away. It was stupid. No, *I* was stupid. I pushed you away and I nearly lost you for good. I don't know if I'm ever going to be able to forgive myself for that."

"I would have gone, anyway. I had my own mission."

"I know, and I wouldn't have stood in your way, but

I may have been able to do something sooner when you were taken into custody."

"You did enough. I'm here, aren't I?"

"You are. I'd like to believe it's for good, but I know I can't expect that of you. But I do want you to know that you will always have a place here with me, whenever you want it. I meant that, Isobel. Whenever, however—you call the shots. I'm yours."

Isobel felt her heart fill at his words. They still had so much to work through but here he was, this proud man, offering her his world.

"I never thought I'd ever want to spend forever with one person, or to have one home base for the rest of my life. I've been traveling for so long now that it's become second nature."

"Maybe sometimes I can come with you."

"I'd like that." She smiled and cupped his face. "I'd like that a lot. And when you can't, I think I'll like coming home to you."

She leaned down and kissed him, savoring the sensation of his lips against hers, of how right it felt to be with him again. When she broke the kiss, she snuggled against him, and they half sat half lay on the sofa in front of the fireplace together, wrapped in one another's arms and their own thoughts. Eventually, Isobel knew she had to tell Ethan how she really felt, about why she'd come back here to The Masters.

"I knew I loved you when I left. It terrified me, in fact. Even though I wanted you to ask me to stay, I think I would have left, anyway." His arms tightened around her but he remained silent and she was grateful for the mental space, the opportunity to regroup her thoughts and deliver them to him as he deserved. "I realize now that it's actually safe to love someone else, to trust them with your heart. No, let me get that right. It's safe for me to love *you*. I know you have the capacity to hurt me, to crush me if you really wanted to, but I also know you couldn't do what you did for me and be someone who would deliberately hurt me at the same time.

"I really struggled with knowing I loved you, but when I was stuck in that prison, in a cell with a couple of dozen other women, each of whom had so much less than me, it was thinking of you, of here, that kept me from losing my mind." She reached up and pushed her fingers through his hair, loving the fact she could do this, that she could feel him with her on so many levels. "Before I left I worried that I didn't fit in here, with you in your home and in your family and in your world. But knowing that you love me makes me understand that I belong with you—that I can finally put down roots, as long as you're with me, too."

"If you'll let me, I will always be with you, Isobel. I don't want to ever let you go again, although I know you'll need to for your work. I can handle waiting for you wherever you go if I know you'll be coming back. Wherever I am will always be your home, too."

"I know that now. I guess I was on the run from commitment because I was just too afraid to trust in anyone else. I told you about my parents, about how they kept my mother's illness from me and about how my dad uprooted me when she died. I never made peace with that and I never, ever wanted to give anyone the capacity to hurt me the way my dad hurt once Mum was gone. It wasn't just them. I saw it over and over again in many of my subjects overseas. For me, it became the face of love, and it wasn't something I was prepared to try—not when it came at such an incredibly high cost."

Ethan sighed and rubbed his hand across her back. "I know what you mean. As much as I loved my father, he was a distant man. He didn't give love easily unless he felt you'd earned it. Maybe that's what drove my mother into another man's arms. Who knows. But despite his distance, I'm sure he loved her in his own way. Sadly, for them, it wasn't enough.

"I spent too many years of my life emulating his example. I don't want to do that anymore. I need to learn to bend and flow a bit more, to share responsibility and to let other people into my life, and particularly into my heart."

Isobel looked up at him. Beneath her ear she heard his heart beat steadily and filled with warmth at the knowledge that it beat for her. "People like me?"

"Definitely you, Isobel. Always you."

He closed his arms tight around her, holding her as if he'd never let her go, and for the first time in her life Isobel didn't feel restrained.

"I thought I'd lose myself if I loved someone like I love you," she said. "But it isn't about losing me at all—it's about filling that part of me that wasn't whole to begin with. You are that person for me, Ethan. I feel whole when I'm with you. I'm only half a person when we're apart. I had to go away to understand that."

Ethan pressed a kiss to her forehead. "If that's the case, then the past couple of months have been worth the agony of waiting to find out if you were ever coming back to me."

"I will always come back to you," she vowed fervently. "But one day, not too far away, I think I'll be ready to settle down, to live a quieter life. One where we can have a family of our own, where we can plan our future together."

"I look forward to that day," Ethan replied. "And in the

meantime, let me show you just how glad I am to know we have that to look forward to."

And he did. All. Night. Long.

* * * * *

COMING NEXT MONTH from Harlequin Desire®
AVAILABLE APRIL 2, 2013

#2221 PLAYING FOR KEEPS

The Alpha Brotherhood

Catherine Mann

Malcolm Douglas uses his secret Interpol connections to protect his childhood sweetheart when her life is in danger. But their close proximity reignites flames they thought were long burned out.

#2222 NO STRANGER TO SCANDAL

Daughters of Power: The Capital

Rachel Bailey

Will a young reporter struggling to prove herself fall for the older single dad who's investigating her family's news network empire—with the intention of destroying it?

#2223 IN THE RANCHER'S ARMS

Rich, Rugged Ranchers

Kathie DeNosky

A socialite running from her father's scandals answers an ad for a mail-order bride. But when she falls for the wealthy rancher, she worries the truth will come out.

#2224 MILLIONAIRE IN A STETSON

Colorado Cattle Barons

Barbara Dunlop

The missing diary of heiress Niki Gerard's mother triggers an all-out scandal. While she figures out who she can trust, the new rancher in town stirs up passions...and harbors secrets of his own.

#2225 PROJECT: RUNAWAY HEIRESS

Project: Passion

Heidi Betts

A fashionista goes undercover to find out who's stealing her company's secrets but can't resist sleeping with the enemy when it comes to her new British billionaire boss.

#2226 CAROSELLI'S BABY CHASE

The Caroselli Inheritance

Michelle Celmer

The marketing specialist brought in to shake up Robert Caroselli's workaday world is the same woman he had a New Year's one-night stand with—and she's pregnant with his baby!

You can find more information on upcoming Harlequin® titles, free excerpts and more at www.Harlequin.com.

HDCNM0313

Midway through the junior high choir's rehearsal of "It's a Small World," Celia Patel found out just how small the world could shrink.

She dodged as half the singers—the female half—sprinted down the stands, squealing in fan-girl glee. All their preteen energy was focused on racing to where he stood.

Malcolm Douglas.

Seven-time Grammy Award winner.

Platinum-selling soft rock star.

And the man who'd broken Celia's heart when they were both sixteen years old.

Malcolm raised a stalling hand to his ominous bodyguards while keeping his eyes locked on Celia, smiling that million-watt grin. Tall and honed, he still had a hometown-boy-handsome appeal. He'd merely matured—now polished with confidence and whipcord muscle.

She wanted him gone.

For her sanity's sake, she *needed* him gone. But now that he was here, she couldn't look away.

He wore his khakis and Ferragamo loafers with the easy confidence of a man comfortable in his skin. Sleeves rolled up on his chambray shirt exposed strong, tanned forearms and musician's hands.

HDEXP0313

Best not to think about his talented, nimble hands.

His sandy-brown hair was as thick as she remembered. It was still a little long, skimming over his forehead in a way that once called to her fingers to stroke it back. And those blue eyes—heaven help her…

There was no denying, he was all man now.

What in the hell was he doing here?

Malcolm hadn't set foot in Azalea, Mississippi, since a judge crony of her father's had offered Malcolm the choice of juvie or military reform school nearly eighteen years ago. Since he'd left her behind—scared, *pregnant* and determined to salvage her life.

But they weren't sixteen anymore, and she'd put aside reckless dreams the day she'd handed her newborn daughter over to a couple who could give the precious child everything Celia and Malcolm couldn't.

She threw back her shoulders and started across the gym.

She refused to let Malcolm's appearance yank the rug out from under her blessedly routine existence. She refused to give him the power to send her pulse racing.

She refused to let Malcolm Douglas threaten the future she'd built for herself.

What is Malcolm doing back in town?

Find out in

PLAYING FOR KEEPS

Available April 2013 from Harlequin® Desire!

HARLEQUIN Desire

ALWAYS POWERFUL, PASSIONATE AND PROVOCATIVE.

When fashionista Lily Zaccaro goes undercover
to find out who's stealing her company's secrets,
she can't resist sleeping with the enemy, her new
British billionaire boss, Nigel Statham.

Look for

PROJECT: RUNAWAY HEIRESS

by Heidi Betts

part of the
Project: Passion miniseries!

Available April 2013 from Harlequin Desire
wherever books are sold.

Project: Passion

On the runway, in the bedroom,
down the aisle—these high-flying
fashionistas mean business.

Powerful heroes…scandalous secrets…burning desires.